Li

The Third Class Genie

Disasters were leading two nil on Alec's disaster–triumph scorecard, when he slipped into the vacant factory lot, locally known as the Tank. Ginger Wallace was hot on his heels, ready to destroy him, and Alec had escaped just in the nick of time. There were disasters awaiting him at home too, when he discovered that he would have to move out of his room and into the boxroom. And, of course, there was school . . .

But Alec's luck changed when he found a beer can that was still sealed, but obviously empty. Stranger still, when he held it up to his ear, he could hear a faint snoring . . . When Alec finally opened the mysterious can, something happened that gave triumphs a roaring and most unexpected lead.

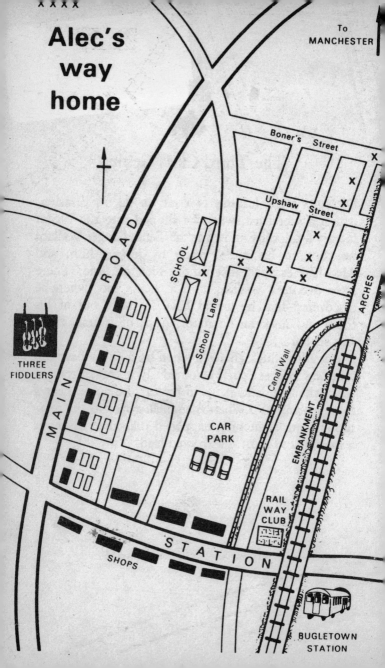

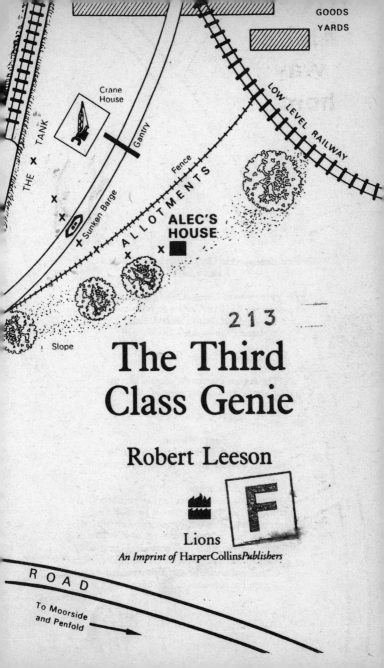

GOODS YARDS

LOW LEVEL RAILWAY

Crane House

Gantry

THE TANK

Fence

ALLOTMENTS

Sunken Barge

ALEC'S HOUSE

Slope

213

The Third Class Genie

Robert Leeson

F

Lions
An Imprint of HarperCollinsPublishers

ROAD

To Moorside and Penfold →

First published in Great Britain in Lions 1975
15 17 19 20 18 16

Lions is an imprint of HarperCollins Children's Books,
a division of HarperCollins Publishers Ltd,
77–85 Fulham Palace Road,
Hammersmith, London W6 8JB

Copyright © Robert A. Leeson 1975

The author asserts the moral right to
be identified as the author of this work

ISBN 0 00 671633-4

Set in Plantin
Printed and bound in Great Britain by
HarperCollins Manufacturing, Glasgow

1

Disasters Two, Triumphs Nil

Mondays are bad enough, any week. But this one broke all records. Alec knew, because he kept a score every day in his head with triumphs on one side and disasters on the other. Today disasters were away down the field while the other team was still in the changing room.

Late as usual, Alec trundled into the schoolyard to join the tail end of line-up. He found himself next to Sam Taylor, which was not a good start to the day. Sam was as thick as a plank and nasty with it, but today he wasn't interested in Alec. His spotty face gleaming, he was studying someone in the line-up, a new lad, tall, broad-shouldered, with a boxer's nose. His face was brown but his short, bristly hair was light red.

"Hey, Ginger," said Sam Taylor.

The boy looked away and said nothing.

"I'm talking to you, Ginger."

The boy turned.

"My name's Wallace, Spotty."

"Oh, beg pardon, Mr Wallace." Sam's voice took on a painful, affected accent. "Tell me, Mr Wallace, how does a gentleman from your part of the Commonwealth come to have ginger hair?"

This time there was no answer. The boy's back was turned once more.

But one of Spotty's mates muttered, "Must have been a red-headed sailor in port." Before he could stop himself, Alec started to snigger. He caught a ferocious look from the red-headed boy and covered up his mouth. Sam and his mates were looking away.

"Very funny, eh?" said Ginger.

Alec began to protest when someone loomed behind him.

It was Monty Cartwright, senior master and keeper of the punishment book, famed for his black beret and habit of ranging the schoolyard as though planning military manoeuvres.

"Quiet in the line-up, Bowden. For someone your size you make an awful lot of noise."

Alec went glumly into school. He knew it was not his day, and he could feel more trouble on the way. He was right: by half-time, disasters had one in the net.

As he wandered into the yard at break, his way was barred by Ginger Wallace.

"Hey, Skinny."

That hurt even if it was true. Alec looked from side to side. There was no escape and no support in sight. He fixed his eye on Ginger's half-knotted tie, because looking up into his face made him feel smaller still.

"I've seen you down Boner's Street, haven't I?"

"Yes," Alec replied before he could stop himself. "My mate lives down there."

"Does he? What number?"

"Number 85."

"No, he doesn't! *We* live at Number 85."

"Well, he used to, but he's moved out to Moorside." That was true, worse luck. Moorside was six miles away and Alec felt friendless.

"OK, so listen, Skinny. You don't come down Boner's Street any more, see?"

Alec swallowed. "I'll . . ."

Ginger interrupted. "You come down Boner's Street, Skinny, and you'll get thumped. It's as simple as that." Ginger walked away, hands in pockets, leaving Alec half scared, half angry.

Later that afternoon was double History and Mr Bakewell let Alec work on his Crusader project. It was nearly finished and Alec had got a lot of fun out of it, but today his mind wasn't on the Crusaders. It was grappling with this latest disaster.

It certainly was a disaster. Boner's Street was his secret short cut home. Everyone else thought Boner's Street came to a dead end by the railway arches, but Alec knew differently. There was more to his secret than just a short cut. No, Ginger Wallace could take a running jump! He was going home down Boner's.

"Hey," whispered Ronnie Carter who sat just in front of him. "That's a sign of old age, talking to yourself."

"Oh, belt up," said Alec.

"Less noise at the back there," warned Mr Bakewell.

Alec gritted his teeth and returned to the Third Crusade. A thought struck him. It was about one hundred yards from the school gate to Boner's Street along School Lane and, if he got away from school sharpish, he might be able to get through Boner's before Ginger Wallace put the barricades up. It was worth a try. He began craftily to slide his books and his project folder into his school bag.

When the pips sounded over the tannoy for the end of school, Alec was away like a rocket and across the schoolyard with the first leavers. At the gate into School Lane he screeched to a halt. Ginger Wallace was already there, sitting on a wall.

"Hey, Skinny," he called. "Don't forget what I said. You stay away from Boner's."

"Oh, leave him," said a tall, bronze-haired girl who was standing next to Ginger.

"Ma wants us home early," she added. Ginger shrugged and they walked away down School Lane. Biting his lip, Alec watched them go while around him the hordes poured out of the schoolyard into the road. Soon Ginger and his sister were out of sight.

Alec waited a few moments, then with his school bag swinging he launched himself across School Lane into Upshaw Street. He ran until the street ended by the high canal wall, then he turned left into a narrow lane, slowing his pace.

This alley, lined with derelict houses and broken-down workshops, led back into Boner's Street.

Above him loomed the railway arches. Most of them were boarded up solidly, with thick tarred planking, which gave the streets a gloomy look. The whole area looked grim, with some parts pulled down, and other parts falling down. Only Boner's Street was more or less intact, with two rows of old three-storey houses, stone steps down to the road and battered stone ornaments on the parapets.

Like Billy the Kid sneaking out of jail while the Sheriff's back is turned, Alec paused by the corner of Boner's and looked round. There was no sign of Ginger Wallace or anyone else coming from the School Lane end. The way seemed clear.

But no. A sudden whistling, squeaking sound made him jump back. He skipped over a low wall at the street corner and crouched down while the squeaking noise came nearer. He peeped over the wall. An old lady was pushing a broken-down pram along the pavement. Alec breathed out. It was only Miss Morris with her load of washing. She was Boner's Street's oldest inhabitant and they had both seen better days. She trundled along dressed in a bright green turban, plastic mac and workman's boots, murmuring to herself. Alec kept out of sight. Miss Morris was an inquisitive old lady and she could easily mention to Mum that one Alec Bowden had been spotted lurking in a suspicious manner near the arches. That could be disastrous.

As she disappeared, Alec got up to cross Boner's Street but flopped down again. He flattened himself to the ground. This meant getting brick dust all over his school trousers, but that was just too bad. He had to stay hidden because the front door of Number 85 opposite had opened and Ginger Wallace stood at the top of the steps, looking up and down the street.

Something was digging into Alec's stomach, half a brick or a can. It hurt, but he dared not move because just then, Ginger crossed the street and stopped only a couple of yards away on the other side of the wall. Alec tried to make himself smaller but whatever was digging into him was killing him. He wriggled a hand under his body and pulled. The object moved and the pain eased. Ginger Wallace, whistling, charged off down the road.

Alec stood up and looked at the object in his hand. It was a can after all, a beer can with a new label. He started to throw it away, then stopped. There was something strange about the can. It was sealed, but it felt light, as though it were empty. How could a can be sealed and yet empty? It was like one of the locked room mysteries.

The road was empty now, except for Alec. He stuffed the intriguing can into his jacket pocket and brushed most of the brick dust off his trousers. Then he picked up his bag and moved slowly, stealthily down the pavement to the bottom of Boner's. Here the railway arch spanning the street towered high above him. Like most of the other arches it was boarded up with thick, blackened planking and nailed to the planks was an old notice which read: BUGLETOWN ORDNANCE: KEEP OUT. Alec began to count the planks until he reached the fourteenth from the right. A few seconds later

Boner's Street was empty again. Alec worked this disappearing trick every afternoon on his way home from school. It was simple, if you knew how. The fourteenth plank was loose enough for him to push it back about nine inches and wriggle through to the other side. There are some advantages in being skinny.

Once through the fence and under the railway arch, Alec was in another world known only to himself. In front of him lay a strip of land, overgrown with elder bushes and rosebay willow herbs, littered with piles of moss-covered bricks, fallen chimneys and rotted rafters. At the centre stood a long low building with great holes in its roof. It was the ruin of an old factory, known locally as the "Tank", though Alec had no idea why. On one side it was cut off by the railway arches and on the other ran the canal, disused now, its black ooze topped with green weed. In one direction the canal vanished under the railway arches; in the other it disappeared among the tangled bushes towards the goods yard and the low level railway, where Alec could hear the distant whistle of shunting engines.

Beyond the canal stood a tall wooden fence, as thick and solid as that which blocked the arches, and beyond the fence lay the estate where Alec's family lived.

From his home you looked down a slope over the allotments and all you could see was this tall fence. People living on the estate, Mum in particular, liked it that way. They didn't want to know about the Tank because it was an eyesore. But Alec didn't care. The Tank was his fortress, his space ship, his hideout where he recovered when life's disasters became too much for him.

To get home, Alec had to cross the canal. He could take the triumphal route, clambering up over the high iron gantry which once supported an overhead crane. Or he could go by the easier route, the one he took when he felt low. Twenty yards down the canal from the main Tank building lay a sunken barge, its timbers just showing above the slime. Alec had fixed loose planks from one timber to another to make a bridge. Today that was his chosen route.

He stopped by the main building to get his breath back and to make one more effort to get the brick dust off his trousers. As he brushed his clothes, his hand knocked against the can in his jacket pocket. He pulled it out and studied it again. It was definitely unopened. The metal seal was intact, but it was as light as a feather. He shook it, but no swishing sounds came forth. He lifted it up to his ear like a seashell. Then he nearly dropped it with surprise. He heard a fantastic sound, not like surf on a distant shore, but like snoring on a nearby bed.

Snoring? Alec took a good grip, shook the can and held it to his ear again. This time there was silence, but he had heard a noise. There was something funny about the can, without a doubt. The only one way to satisfy his curiosity was to open it; though perhaps he could save that as a treat for later on.

While he hesitated, his mind was made up for him. From the railway arch came the rumble of a train and a long drawn-out blast from its hooter: "Da-da-da-daaaa". Alec stuffed the can in his pocket, picked up his bag and ran down to the canal. That signal meant only one thing. Dad was bringing the 3.30 diesel from Manchester into Bugletown Station. "Da-da-da-daaaa" was a message to Mum: "Put the kettle on, I'll be home by five o'clock." It meant the time was already twenty-to-five and if Flash Bowden wasn't in re-entry orbit soon, there'd be a cosmic disaster.

And there was.

In his haste to cross the canal, Alec never noticed that one of his planks was out of place, or rather, he noticed it as his foot was on the way down. He did an imitation jungle dance in the air, as he tried to jump over to the farther side, but the distance was too great. One foot landed safely on the bank but the other plunged down into five fathoms of black, green, greasy canal gunge.

"Oh, Nora," groaned Alec, "Disasters two, triumphs nil."

2

"Elephant's nest up a rhubarb tree"

Knee-deep in the canal, Alec grabbed wildly for the weeds and grass that grew on the bank. He lost hold of his school bag. His first clutch was on a bunch of nettles. He yelled, dropped back and grabbed again. This time, he dragged himself on to the bank with a great heave and sat down to work out how much damage had been done. It was a disaster all right. His trouser leg was coated in thick greasy slime up to the knee and so were his sock and trainer. He had to admit that he smelt terrible. He suddenly saw his bag slowly sinking out of sight into the ghastly depths of the canal. Lying flat on the towpath, he stretched out his arm and just managed to reach the handle and pull the bag out. The canal, reluctant to let go, made a rude, sucking noise.

Alec stood up and did his best to clean the satchel, which was fairly easy, and then his clothes, which was more difficult. A handful of grass took off the worst, but five minutes of frantic rubbing still left his trousers looking grotty and smelling worse. "Bowden," he muttered, "you've put your foot in it."

There was nothing to do but go home. His arrival would be at the most disastrous time, with Dad (saying nothing, but looking grim), Mum (looking grim and saying a lot) and his sister Kim, home from the biscuit works (laughing her head off). But there was no getting out of it. Forward, Bowden!

He crossed the waste ground to the fence. Here again, he carefully counted the boards to find the loose one only he knew about, pushed it forward. With a grunt and wriggle he was out at the foot of the slope below the council houses. No one was about, though it was a fine evening. From the windows came the white glow of televisions switched on, the clatter of cups and plates, and other pleasant sounds of people enjoying their tea without a care in the world.

Was there a chance, Alec wondered as he reached the bottom of his street, of getting in through the front door and sneaking straight upstairs to his bedroom, so avoiding the kitchen and the reception committee? It was a wild hope, he knew. Front doors on the estate were opened twice in a lifetime, for weddings and funerals, and to go in that way would be impossible without knocking. So it was round the corner of the house to the kitchen door. Alec braced himself to go in.

"Psst, Alec lad."

The voice came from the green and white caravan parked in the back yard. One side rested on a wheel, the other side rested on a pile of bricks built up under the axle. Dad was always threatening to mend it, but never did. The small side window of

15

the caravan opened and a round, red face with wild, white hair peered out.

"Alec lad. What have you done?"

Alec relaxed.

"Oh, Granddad, you made me jump."

"I don't wonder. You were trying to sneak in, weren't you?"

Alec nodded.

Granddad's face disappeared from the window and the caravan door opened. An arm stretched out, beckoning, and Alec, with one eye on the kitchen door, slunk in, while Granddad closed the caravan door after him.

Inside the heat was terrific and the air was blue with pipe smoke and foul with the fumes of an old oil heater. More heat came from a small soldering iron which was slowly growing red at the side of the fire. Through the fog Alec could see Granddad perched on one of the bunks. His thin old body was dressed in the remains of a braided dressing-gown and a pair of striped pyjamas. Displaying a row of broken teeth he grinned at Alec. On the folding table next to the bed were a plate, a loaf of bread, a half-opened tin of pilchards and a jug of beer.

"Hallo, Granddad, what are you soldering?" asked Alec, forgetting his troubles for a moment.

"I'm not soldering, you daft ha'porth, I'm mulling," replied Granddad, and with that he seized the hot soldering iron and plunged it hissing into the beer jug. A cloud of steam and a strange smell rose to join the general fug inside the little room. Granddad held up the jug.

16

"Want a taste?" he asked, but Alec shook his head hastily.

Granddad poured himself a glass, drank deeply and then wiped his mouth primly on a paper handkerchief he took from his dressing-gown sleeve.

"Now, lad, if you'll give me your breeches, I'll clean 'em up for you. I can see you've been in the canal. Don't argue. Take your trainers off and put them by the fire here, while I use the meths on your other clothes."

"But Granddad," Alec protested.

"By the time we've done that, you can sneak in through the kitchen because they'll all be in the front room."

"How do you know, Granddad?"

"Because there's trouble, that's why. Your brother Tom, his wife and the baby are going to move back in with us. They've lost their place and that means rearrangements and people shifting round."

Alec's heart sank. This was truly the most disastrous day he had ever suffered. For the news meant one thing to him. Tom and his family would be given the second bedroom, Kim would have to move into Alec's little bedroom at the back, and that meant Alec would be moved up to the boxroom. For anyone who thinks a boxroom is place where you keep boxes, it's not. A boxroom is a room like a box; it's a space at the top of the stairs, with a door to stop the bed from falling downstairs. It's a place where they train men for working in midget submarines. Alec had slept in the boxroom for years until brother Tom moved out. Now, disaster of disasters, he would have to lose his own bedroom and go back there.

Granddad stretched out a thin hand and ruffled his hair. "Come on, lad. Cheer up. There's plenty worse off. Give us your trousers." Alec handed them over and sat up on the other bunk while Granddad got out a bottle of methylated spirits and set to work rubbing the stains on Alec's trousers. As he worked, the old man began to sing, half under his breath.

> *"Oh, the elephant is a dainty bird,*
> *It flits from bough to bough,*
> *It builds its nest in a rhubarb tree,*
> *And whistles like a cow."*

As Grandad sang, thoughts of disaster began to fade from Alec's mind . . .

> *"Ha, ha, ha, hee, hee, hee . . .*
> *Elephant's nest up a roobub tree,*
> *Ha, ha, ha, hee, hee, hee . . ."*

Suddenly Granddad sniffed.

"There's a funny smell in here, lad."

Alec stared.

"You must be joking, Granddad. There're fifty funny smells in here."

"Nay, lad, an extra funny smell. Oh, Lord, your trainers!"

Granddad dropped the rag he was using to clean Alec's trousers and turned to the oil stove from which a thick brown haze was rising.

"Oh no!" cried Alec.

Oh no, indeed. Half the side of one of his trainers was burned through and the other one was singed. Granddad saved Alec's sock with a quick snatch but the damage was done. Life, thought Alec, had become a disaster area.

"Don't fret, lad. I'll tell your Mum what happened and buy you another pair," said Granddad.

"No, you won't," protested Alec. He wouldn't let Granddad spend his pension on new trainers. "I'll have to tell Mum myself. Perhaps I'll get our Kim to lend me some cash and buy myself a pair."

"Anyway, lad, your trousers are all right now. But don't stand too close to the stove when you put them on or you'll go up in smoke."

Alec dressed quickly, said cheerio, and walked into the kitchen with a shuffle that more or less hid the burnt side of his trainer. The kitchen was empty, as Granddad had predicted, but from the front room came the low sound of voices. Alec crept quietly towards the passage. If he could reach the stairs without . . .

"Alec," came his mother's voice. "Is that you, Alec?"

"Yes," muttered Alec.

"Listen, love. We're busy in here. There's a bit of meat pie and tomato on top of the fridge. You can have that for your tea."

"Can I take it up to my room?" asked Alec, unable to believe his luck.

"All right, but don't make a mess."

Alec crept up the stairs with a plate in one hand and his satchel in the other and did not breathe again until he was safely inside his bedroom. It was small, but a palace compared with the box-room. It had his own bed, a battered old desk Dad had picked up at a jumble sale, a chair and a cupboard full of all his most precious odds and ends. They'd have to go down into the shed if he moved into the boxroom, thought Alec gloomily, as he sat down on the bed and began to eat his meat pie.

As he ate, he started to make up his final triumph–disaster scoreboard for the day. He didn't write it down, because things like that are highly confidential, but he made it up in his mind like this:

1. Ginger Wallace is out to thump me.
2. Ginger Wallace is trying to stop me going home down Boner's Street.
3. Ginger Wallace might find out about the Tank.
4. I've ruined my trainers.
5. No pocket money for a month.
6. I have to move back into the boxroom.
7. I'm in the doghouse with Monty Cartwright.

He thought over the list carefully. Had he missed anything out? There's nothing worse than a disaster that sneaks up on you. No, they were all there. The next question was had he made the list too long? Was Ginger Wallace really three disasters?

Alec didn't hesitate; Ginger Wallace was at least three disasters.

Strictly speaking, numbers four and five were just one disaster. That is, five couldn't be a disaster but for four. Life without trainers is hard. Life without pocket money is disastrous.

Number six was a disaster all right. It hadn't happened yet, but neither had one, two or three, and that didn't make him feel any better. Number seven he decided to cross off the list. After the telling-off in line-up that day he'd heard no more and Mr Cartwright did not usually brood over past crimes. So that made the score six so far, or five if you counted numbers four and five as one. Five for disasters so far, while the other side hadn't even crossed the half-way line.

It was the highest score for disasters since that black day when he'd got all his homeworks mixed up and collected five detentions in a row. As he thought of this, his eye fell on his school bag. He should really take a last look at his history project on the Crusades before he handed it in tomorrow. He tipped out his books on to the bed and for the thirty-fourth time that day, his heart stopped.

Across the cover of his history project was a green stain. He opened the cover. Almost every page was a sodden green wreck with drawings, cut-outs, and writing all awash with Bugletown Canal gunge. This must have seeped through the side of his bag where the stitching had given way.

It would take ages to look up all that stuff again, let alone write it. That made disasters leading six nil. Almost a rugby score. Was there nothing today remotely like a triumph? He thought for a while.

21

There was that funny, sealed but empty, beer can he had found in Boner's Street. He could investigate that.

Bowden, he said to himself, you're entitled to a treat. Give yourself the evening off. Tomorrow's a disaster from the word go. Let's save what we can of today. With that he jumped from the bed, took off his school clothes, put on his old jumper and jeans and quietly opened the bedroom door. As he crept down the stairs he heard them still at it in the front room. No trouble at all to sneak out.

"Alec, is that you?" called his mother.

"Yes, Mum. I'm just going out for a bit."

"What about your homework?"

"I've just got some work left to do on my history project, and I'll do that when I get back." Alec always had trouble telling complete porkies.

"No telly then, mind you."

"Shan't want any."

"What's the matter with Mastermind?" That was Kim's mocking voice.

Alec thought of a crushing retort, then remembered that he'd have to ask Kim for a loan. So with a "won't be long", he shot through the back door and was out in the street before you could say antidisestablishmentarianism!

Holding firmly on to his jeans pocket, where the can was wedged rather awkwardly, he ran down the slope and past the allotments. To his surprise, there was Granddad digging away, dressed in his old black suit. Alec waved, but did not stop, and

22

headed for the tall fence round the Tank. If Grand-dad saw him slip through the loose planking, the old man gave no sign.

Alec paused for a second inside the fence, as he always did, to run his eye over the little kingdom amid its silent wilderness of elder bushes and weeds. The setting sun flashed on one of the few panes left in the window of the crane house, and cast giant shadows between the crumbling ivy-covered walls. Alec was heading for the canal when he remembered that the plank had collapsed under him that after-noon. He would have to cross by the old travelling crane gantry and enter the crane room through the window. Although this was a day of disaster and it seemed unsuitable to take the triumphal route, he couldn't be bothered to find a new plank for his bridge just now. He turned right and ran along the towpath to the gantry.

Climbing the uprights by the steel steps was easy enough; the difficult part was when you had to cross the girder fifteen feet up above the canal. One false move and you would never be seen again. The safest but slowest way was to straddle the iron and edge your way over a foot at a time. The quickest and riskiest way was to balance on the six-inch-wide girder and walk boldly over like a tight-rope man. Crouching and waddling like a duck, Alec settled for a mixture of the two. Halfway over, it became easier because of the iron arm of an old hand crane which stretched alongside the main gantry.

At last he was across and wriggling his way through the broken window of the crane room.

He put one foot on the lever and chain drum which were still linked to the hand crane and then he was down on the floor. He gave a jump and skip and looked around him. Now he was in command. He turned and faced the canal, peering through the dusty broken window. Then he seized the hand crane lever and slowly pushed it forward. He had spent many a Saturday afternoon greasing and oiling the mechanism, so that it moved. With a rattle the chain began to run through the pulley at the end of the crane and drop towards the canal. Alec threw the brake and stopped the chain just above the water. Then he bent down to the drum and taking the handle, carefully wound the chain up again.

When he worked the hand crane, he could imagine anything. He was loading a ship, rescuing a trapped submarine crew, hauling up treasure from a mine, replacing the piles in a nuclear reactor. He finished winding in the chain and put on the brake. Then he heaved himself on to the table and sat a moment looking out of the crane room window.

Now he was ready to investigate the mystery of the sealed, empty can.

"The question is, Watson, not why the can was empty, but why it was sealed?"

"Amazing, Holmes, I mean, Bowden. But what is the answer?"

"I'll have to open it, won't I, you plonker?"

Alec held up the can and inspected it. Then he raised it once more to his ear, as he had done that afternoon.

It was fantastic. There was the same noise, a sort of growling as though someone were snoring. It was crazy. Alec shook the can and again the noise stopped.

He slipped his finger into the metal ring at the top of the can and pulled. At first it would not budge. Alec tumbled from the table, placed the can on the floor, held it down with one hand, and pulled at the ring again.

There came a sudden tremendous whistling rush of air, like Concorde landing, and a voice thundered . . .

"Alec!"

3

Are you sitting comfortably?

"Alec!"

Alec fell off the crane room table and looked round in amazement. The can, now opened, rolled to and fro on the floor, making cronking noises. But there was no one in sight.

"Who said 'Alec'?" he squeaked.

There was silence. Then Alec got back his normal voice and repeated: "Who called my name?"

No answer. Alec carefully picked up the can and shook it. No snoring sounds. Nothing. But someone had definitely called his name, as well as made noises like Concorde. His ears were still buzzing. He tiptoed to the door and pushed it open to look down the rickety stairs to the ruins of the main factory. Nothing in sight. Shoving the creaking door back into place, Alec came back to the table and looked once more at the strange can standing upright there.

"I must be going round the twist. All these disasters have finally been too much for me. I was sure someone shouted 'Alec'."

"Ah, ing'lizi walad. You English."

Alec leapt away from the can, as the voice

boomed out again. It was like the school tannoy, when Mr Cartwright did his "do-not-resist-or-you-will-be-annihilated" routine.

"Yes, of course, I'm English. But who are you?" said Alec, still alarmed.

"I am slave of lamp – sorry, jug, no, sorry, plate . . . I don't know . . ." The booming voice faded away.

"Don't go," cried Alec.

"I don't go. Worse luck," the voice gave a hiccup.

"Why, what's wrong?"

"Aiee, well may you ask." The voice faded away again muttering in a language Alec could not understand.

"You're not the slave of the lamp, you're the slave of the beer can," he said. Then he had an inspiration. "If you come out of the can, you'd feel better and your voice wouldn't sound so funny."

There was a fizzing sound, another burst of hiccups and a pop.

"Shukran jazilan, Effendi."

"No need to be offended," replied Alec, who had now got into the swing of the game, whatever the game was. Whoever it might be speaking to him, it was good fun and a change from the gloom and misery of the day so far.

"Not offended, Effendi. Effendi, Master."

"Oh, don't call me master," said Alec. "It reminds me of school. Besides," he went on, "you started calling me Alec. Can't you carry on like that? It's more friendly."

"Alec?" the voice was puzzled.

"Yes. When I opened the beer can, you said 'Alec'."

The voice began to laugh.

"Not 'Alec'. I said, 'Salaam Aleikum, peace be with you!'"

"That's nice," said Alec. "I could use some peace just now."

"May your enemies be destroyed, your crops increase, your camels grow fat and your wives never quarrel."

"Well, thanks very much, or what was it you said? Shukran jazilan. But my troubles aren't quite like that," said Alec.

"Tell me, O master, and they shall vanish like dust before the khamsin wind."

"Oh, great," said Alec. "You are just what I need. But please don't call me master. My name's Alec. And, by the way, what is your name? And just how do you come to be hiding inside a beer can?"

There was silence for some moments, then a sigh.

"If my master – Alec – is sitting comfortably, I will begin."

Alec hoisted himself on to the table and sat down.

"Know, Alec, that my name is Abu Salem, Genie of the Third Order of rank and merit in the courts of Baghdad, Damascus and Cairo, one of the slaves of the lamp."

"But, Abu," interrupted Alec, "there was only one slave of the lamp."

"In the days of Aladdin, that was true. But the story does not end there. For when Aladdin became

Sultan and the wealthiest man in the world, the magician who was his enemy decided to take his revenge. He used his magic powers to make hundreds of small lamps, each one with a third-rank genie, and he gave these to people in the city.

"Instead of working, all these people began to use their magic lamps to make gold, food or clothes, as they fancied. Soon it seemed that everyone in the kingdom was imitating Sultan Aladdin. There was so much gold that no one cared for it any more and they used it to make buckets and feeding troughs. Aladdin became furious and, thinking that the world was laughing at him, sent his soldiers to seize the lamps and to melt them down.

"But now the people became furious too. They said, 'If our lamps shall melt, so shall yours.' Aladdin had to agree. So all the lamps were melted down, and the great lump of metal was put into the palace storeroom and forgotten.

"Many many years later, when all this had been forgotten and Aladdin was no more than a story for children, there was a great war. The metal in the storeroom was made into shot for cannons and fired from the palace walls. Some landed in the sand and was forgotten again and some was buried in the ruins of the palace. Only a few pieces were found. One was used by a poor man to hold open his door and for all I know the genie sleeps within it to this day. Happy man.

"But one was found by a metal-smith who used it to make a jug. With the handling and knocking and rubbing and polishing of daily use, the genie within it awoke. That unlucky spirit, O Alec, was I."

Alec leaned forward. He wasn't quite sure where Abu the genie might be, in spirit so to speak, so he spoke to the beer can.

"How long did all this take?"

"I know not. A few hundred years perhaps. This time the owner was a poor man, like Aladdin in the beginning, and being poor, he was hungry too. When first I told him to make his wish, he asked for food. And food I brought him. Soon, he who had been poor and hungry became rich and very fat. And being rich, he was also vain, and being vain, he wished he were not fat."

"So, couldn't you help him lose weight?" demanded Alec.

"Indeed, I could and so I did. He became as light as a feather, but, alas, he said nothing about size. Thus, he rose in the air, like a balloon, and the east wind carried him slowly away over the mountains and he was never seen again.

"It has been my fate, O Alec, to give my masters what they did not want. Be warned. Be warned."

"Oh, I'll take my chance," said Alec. "Go on, what happened next?"

"The jug which had brought such evil into the house was cast out. I slept happily on the rubbish dumps of old Baghdad for a few centuries more. Ah, what bliss . . ." The voice yawned, and for a moment Alec feared that Abu might go to sleep again. But no.

"I was found by a scavenger who sold me with some other vessels to a smith, who again melted down the metal and made plates. This time I was bought in the local bazaar by a British soldier who planned to polish the plate and send it home to his wife.

"Awakened once more from my sleep, I was at his command. His first order was that I should make him colonel of the regiment and this I did. He immediately turned the officer who had commanded the regiment into a private soldier. Indeed, when I saw the transformations which he brought about, I knew I had met my match.

"Next he commanded the officers of the regiment to do all the duties of the camp. They had to stand guard at night, to make food in the cookhouse, and to polish the great brass cannon that stood at the camp gate. The sergeants of the regiment were made to serve the private soldiers with tea in bed each morning, to press their uniforms and clean their equipment.

"For weeks the soldiers of the camp enjoyed the life of idleness, but soon news of the strange happenings in the regiment reached London. A high-ranking officer was sent to put matters right, or wrong, if you look at it through the eyes of my master.

"But he outwitted them. He rubbed on the plate, called me to his aid and made himself a general. Then he ordered the regiment home to England, much to the joy of the soldiers. But he had been too clever. Unless he could find someone of higher rank to order him home, he had to remain a soldier. His one hope was to find an accomplice. The only man left was the former colonel whom my master had confined to camp for his rude and impudent behaviour. My master offered him his freedom and also to make him field marshal, if he would give the order that would send my master home. Alas for human wickedness and folly! No sooner was his prisoner made field marshal, than my master was once again made a private and confined to camp, where he was ordered to stand guard at night, make food in the cookhouse and polish the great brass cannon at the camp gate. For all I know, they may still be there in that lonely desert camp."

"But what about you?" demanded Alec.

"Did I not speak of human wickedness? Another soldier, having seen the plate and admired it, took it with him when the regiment sailed for England. He gave it to his wife but she believed that eating from metal plates was bad for the digestion and gave the plate to the passing rag and bone man in exchange for two goldfish, a balloon for her baby and a pair of silk stockings for herself."

"But how did you come to be in the beer can?" insisted Alec.

"Alas, I know not, neither care I. I know that my pleasant sleep is at an end and I have a new master whom I must serve according to the rules of the Order of Genies, Third Class."

"Well, don't look at it like that," said Alec. "I won't ask you to do daft things like the others did."

"Speak not too soon, O Alec. But as you will, so must I do. What is thy will, O Alec?"

"First of all, I want to see who I'm talking to."

"Your wish cannot, alas, be granted. As a genie of the Third Rank, I have not the power to appear and disappear as well as perform tasks. Ask me another."

"How about something smashing to eat? Like a Super Atomic Blast Sherbet Bag?"

"Sherbet," replied Abu, "is not food."

"Food, ah, food . . ." Alec could almost imagine Abu rubbing his stomach. "Food!" The voice rose to a roar.

"Go easy," said Alec, "you'll have half of Bugletown round here in a minute."

Abu laughed. "None can hear me but you, O Alec. But food, ah food . . ."

"Get on with it," said Alec in desperation.

"Food."

Out of the air came a white sheet that spread itself over the dusty crane room table. Abu began to chant . . .

"Nazin Tofa, eggs in wine sauce; Toyla Shorbasi, soup from Paradise; Uskumru Pilaksi, baked mackerel; Kirasili Sulun, pheasant with cherries," he went on as the dishes, steaming and bubbling, began to crowd the cloth.

"Hold on," said Alec, "what about the pud?"

"Ah, Sutlach Sharapli; rice pudding with wine."

Oh, no, not rice pudding! Just like school dinner, thought Alec. But he didn't wish to offend Abu and so he simply invited him to join the meal. Abu

33

readily agreed; several centuries in a jug or a beer can make anyone peckish. Alec stared as the various dishes rose in the air, emptied themselves and then floated down to the table again. But he was busy enjoying the feast himself. So this is what it was like in the days of the Arabian Nights. Oh, clever stuff, Bowden.

Soon the meal was over, and Alec noticed that it was growing dark outside.

"Time we were getting home, Abu."

He had barely time to pick up the can, when the table cloth, table, crane room and all had vanished with a rush and he was back in his bedroom again, sitting on the bed, still in his school uniform.

Had he been sitting there all the time? He looked out of the bedroom window. The sky was clear and down in the yard he could hear Granddad pottering about in the caravan. But the can was in his pocket and it was open.

4

Keeper of the Kan

Baffled and bewildered, Alec held the can in his hands. Was he dreaming? Was Alec Bowden truly the master of Abu Salem, Genie Third Class, approximately 975 years old? Or was Alec Bowden off his trolley? Had the strain of the day been too much? There were his trainers with a big hole burnt in them by helpful old Granddad. There was his project on the Crusades, all soaked in eau de Canal. The disasters were real enough. But what about the triumph?

He held up the can to the light; it gleamed. He held it to his nose; it smelt beery. He held it to his ears and heard a distinct snoring sound. That could mean only one thing. Abu was sleeping off that enormous meal. Was it mackerel and rice pudding, or pheasants and sherbet? Still the memory was clear. His mouth watered.

He rubbed the can briskly and held it up again. The snoring had stopped. He rubbed it again. No sign. Inspiration struck him. Bending his mouth close to the can opening, he said firmly, "Salaam Aleikum, O Abu Salem."

The familiar voice repeated sleepily, "Peace to you, Keef Haalak, How are you?"

"I am well, apart from about two thousand problems," said Alec.

"Aieee, I feared as much. No peace for the genie. Speak, O Alec. What is thy will?"

"My first will is a new pair of trainers."

"Trainers? What are trainers?"

"Slippers."

In a flash the scorched trainers had vanished from Alec's feet, and were instantly replaced by the most elegant pair of pink and gold, plush, satin slippers with curled toes.

"You Great Arabian Plonker," said Alec, "you'll have me drummed out of the Third Year!"

"Are the slippers not to your liking?" Abu sounded a little offended.

"They're lovely, they're gorgeous, but they're not me," said Alec. "I want rubber-soled PE shoes."

"What is rubber?"

"Good grief," said Alec. Then he thought. What is rubber? How do you make it? How do you explain it to a 975-year-old genie, who hasn't had the benefits of Western civilization? All he could remember was a description of plantation life in his geography book. He told Abu. Immediately in front of him there was a tall smooth-trunked tree, standing in the middle of the room, with white liquid seeping from a cut in the bark and flowing down on to the bedroom floor. Alec bent down and poked the liquor which seemed to be setting like a jelly. Now, what to do? For the life of him, he couldn't remember the next stage in rubber-making.

36

Did you fry it, or hang it out of the window, or beat it? He wished he'd listened properly in geography or chemistry.

"Ah well, Abu," he said, "let's have my old trainers back. I'll have to buy a new pair."

"Thy will is my command," said Abu, as though he'd worked miracles.

"Now, you see my project book over there on the bed. I want it cleaned up."

For a second the project book vanished, or seemed to. Then it reappeared. But what had that raving genie done now? The front of the book and the first ten pages, which had been stained with canal mud, had been cleaned up. They'd been wiped clean, completely. There was nothing on them.

"Put it back, Abu, put it back," he yelled.

There was silence for a second.

"Come on, genie-us," demanded Alec, "make with the project."

From the front room Alec's mother knocked on the ceiling.

"A bit less noise up there, our Alec."

Alec groaned. Then Abu said hesitantly, "I fear I cannot put back what you wrote. For I cannot know what it might have been."

Alec stared. That hadn't occurred to him. It wasn't Abu who was daft; it was he. He'd just have to be more careful what he asked. Abu had warned him about all the disasters that had happened to his previous masters.

"It was a story of the Crusades," he said.

"Crusades?"

"When King Richard and the other knights went out to the Holy Land to drive out the Saracens and fought Saladin."

"Aha, Sultan Salah ad-Din Yusuf, Lord of Ishshaan, mighty hammer of the faithless. Who does not know that great story?"

"Do you? It took me an awful time to look it up in the school library. If I have to do all that again . . ."

"Fear not, Alec. Take up thy pen. I shall tell, you shall write and the empty pages shall be full once more with great truth. Let us begin with the mighty victory for the true faith at the battle of Hattin . . ."

Alec rushed to his desk, got out his fountain pen, and began to write, while Abu tirelessly told of sieges, battles, storms of arrows, flash of scimitar and sword, thunder of hooves, and burning sand and sun. There was still much to tell when Alec had filled up the blank space in his project book. But his mother knocked on the ceiling again which was the signal for him to get ready for bed. Outside it was dark now and Alec was tired, but he felt happy again. His project was rescued. True, his trainers were still in a disastrous state, but surely with Abu's aid he could put that right.

Now that he had Abu Salem, genie of the light brown ale on his side, nothing was too much. From now on, triumphs would hammer disasters ten nil every day. Thanks to Abu. Good old Abu.

"Well, Abu, I'm off to bed, if you'd like to climb back into your can. I'll leave the lid up slightly to give you some fresh air. It must smell like a brewery in there. Cheerio for now."

"Ma'asalaama," murmured Abu.

Alec undressed, wandered out to the bathroom to brush his teeth, but at the top of the stairs he stopped. He could hear his mother and father talking in the kitchen where they were having a cup of cocoa.

"I don't know, Connie love. It doesn't matter how you switch around those bedrooms, we haven't really got room."

"Well, I'm fed up with it, Harold. For one reason or another we've never had enough room."

"We could get a four-bedroomed house if we moved out to Moorside."

"The only way you'll get me to Moorside is to carry me in a coffin. Miles from anywhere, freezing cold in winter . . ."

"All right, all right, Connie. Anyway, let's get to bed. Is our Kim in yet?"

"Not her, still, she's got the back door key."

Alec heard them move their chairs down in the kitchen and shot quickly back into his own bedroom. He switched off the light and looked out of the window. The railway arch loomed up against the skyline; the Tank, hidden in the dark shadows of the arch, could not be seen. But Alec knew it was there. He had his hideout, and his new friend Abu. Ginger Wallace, Mr Cartwright and all infidels would bite the dust from now on. Flash Bowden, Scourge of the Cosmos, Defender of the Faith, Keeper of the Kan, was on the warpath.

He tucked the can carefully under his pillow and went to sleep.

5

Bowden the Beast

Alec dreamt that he sat at a huge table in the state-room of his elegant 20,000-ton yacht, as it floated at anchor in the Bugletown Canal. Through the porthole he could see the mate, Monty Cartwright, urging on his trusty crew. The stateroom door opened and Ginger Wallace, in steward's uniform, entered bowing and scraping.

"Alec," he said.

"Admiral Bowden to you," replied Alec and dismissed Ginger with a wave of his hand.

But Ginger would not go. He shouted, "Alec!"

Alec waved his hand irritably, but Ginger only went on shouting, louder and louder. Then Alec was awake and his mother was banging on the bedroom door.

"Alec, it's half past eight!"

"HALF PAST EIGHT?"

At times like this, Alec wished he were an octopus. He'd put on his shoes with one hand (or tentacle), his trousers on with another, wash his face with a third, eat his breakfast with a fourth, pack his school bag with the fifth, tie his tie with the sixth, while the other two were busy walking down to Station Road. Mr Jameson, the biology teacher, once said that an octopus brain was just as good as a human brain. If they'd come to live on land there'd be no doubt about who would be boss.

Alec tumbled down the stairs, dressing as he went. He grabbed his breakfast and shot out of the back door and up the road with his shirt-tail flapping, shoelaces flying and school bag swinging. He was down the hill, turning right into Station Road, and almost under the railway bridge, when a ghastly thought stopped him in his tracks. He'd forgotten his can. Forgotten your can? Bowden, you can't have? I have, you know. Well, go back for it. Don't be daft, it's nearly nine o'clock.

It was no good. He had to go on. Disasters were leading triumphs one nil and the referee's coin was still in the air. Abu Salem, who ought by rights to be straining at the leash with the latest instamatic miracle, was probably lying snoring away with his tin blanket wrapped round him and dreaming of happy days in old Baghdad. "What a life."

Alec must have spoken out loud, because the newspaper seller by the station entrance called out, "The first eighty years are the worst, lad."

He caught the tail end of line-up in the school yard. He saw the broad shoulders of Ginger Wallace going in through the main door a little way ahead of him. Luckily, although they were in the same year (which was a laugh since Ginger was twice Alec's size), they weren't in the same class.

Alec had time to nip along to the History

41

Department and hand in his project to Mr Bakewell, who greeted him with, "Ah, here comes Bowden, at the last minute like the US Cavalry. This ought to be good."

Then on into Assembly, with a mind-bending lecture from the Head about Pride in Appearance and School Reputation. Alec looked down at himself and wondered if he should volunteer to go on display as an example of "How to get the school a bad name". Without thinking he bent down to fasten up his shoelaces. Someone gently pushed him forward and he toppled through the row in front into the middle of the third year girls. There were squeals and chuckles, whispers of "Here comes the Midnight Prowler" and "Bowden the Beast in Human Form", cut short as Miss Bentley came zooming in from the sidelines.

"Get back to your place!"

Alec slunk back. The Head, unaware of the drama beneath him, droned on while Alec tried to make himself smaller. He was in the middle of planning to sneak out of school, go home, wake up Abu, and arrange a quick transfer to a desert island, when he was given a good-humoured shove by the boy next to him and realized that everyone was peeling off for lessons. Double English. Alec did a quick check. What had he forgotten? He couldn't remember.

He was in luck. The English teacher, Miss Welch, Raquel as the boys of 3F called her, looked as though she had been on the tiles the night before. She was clearly in no better shape for the morning than Alec was. That was a thought. Supposing teachers' days were full of disasters as well. Was there no escape, even when you left school and grew up? Maybe Miss Welch would like to be on a desert island right now. Alec's eyes shone with sympathy, but she was quite unaware of it. In fact, she didn't even seem to see him as she drifted round the room, handing out tatty-backed books.

"Read the story starting on page 41 to yourselves and then write it up in your own words."

"Miss," shouted a boy at the back of the class.

"Yes, I know. Yours hasn't got a page 41. Well, try the next story. I don't suppose in your version it will make much difference."

She turned on the class like a swivel gun and added, "And anyone else who hasn't got a page 41 or a page 85 or page 2001 can do likewise. I don't want a peep out of you for the next three days."

That raised a slight laugh and things settled down. The morning got going and Alec was grateful to go along with it. He looked at the story on page 41, but didn't take to it and read on. Next came a chapter from *Treasure Island*. He enjoyed it so much that he read on and on and on. The pips went as he dreamed his way through to page 120.

People were on their feet all round him, handing in their books. Alec hadn't written a word. He fiddled with his books, trying to sort out his mind and bring it back to earth, while the others piled out of the room. Miss Welch stood over him.

"If I did my duty, I'd make you write out your own version of every story you've read this morning, but I'm too soft-hearted. Write up the one on page 41 tonight and hand it to me tomorrow. Now get off to science before I get blamed for hanging on to you."

Alec skidded out. The rest of the morning lumbered along. The lunch break lurked ahead. Alec looked out of the window and vaguely hoped for rain. Not a chance. Outside the sun shone and the yard was filling up with its usual swarm of boys. Alec sidled off to the library and asked the librarian if she wanted any stock-taking done, but his offer was politely declined. Slowly, like a worm watching for early blackbirds, Alec made his way out.

But luck hadn't died on him. A game of backers was going on among the third-year boys by the school field railings and Ginger Wallace and his mates were busy with that. Fascinated, Alec drew nearer and watched as his beefy foe charged and leapt with full weight on his groaning opponents. As Ginger landed, the other team gave up the ghost and collapsed on the ground in howls of pain, while Ginger, straddling an opponent's back, made whooping noises like a demented cowboy. In a moment a new game was lined up and the running, jumping, straining and heaving began again.

Alec quickly stole away, found a corner within a discreet distance of the duty master and joined a civilized game of cobs with a couple of boys he knew slightly.

Whistles blew for line-up and he realized with relief that the lunch hour had passed and Ginger

44

Wallace had forgotten him. Luck was still holding. Maybe he was going to be permanently lucky now that he had the can. If that were so, then why had he forgotten the can? Still, so far so good, he thought as he joined the line-up. Inside the school in the corridor a group of girls shoved past him. One cried out, "There he is. Bowden the brute. No girl's safe from him."

He looked up and caught the flash of white teeth, as Ginger Wallace's sister went by, laughing with her friends. He blushed and pretended to make a close study of the wall, but he felt cheered up as he went in for history.

HISTORY.

That's it. His run of luck was about to fade away. He knew this as soon as he saw, in the classroom, not Mr Bakewell, but Tweedy Harris. It was whispered that as a baby Harris's mother had used powdered chalk on his nappies instead of talcum powder and this had soured him for life. For some reason today he was smiling, though to Alec it looked like the grin on the face of a well-fed boa constrictor.

"History projects – aah – yes," rasped Mr Harris. "Throughout the year I try to tell you a little of the history of this green and pleasant land of ours. And towards the end of the year, you generously agree to set down on paper what you have understood of it. One of the exciting things about my work," Tweedy paused as his audience waited for the catch-line, "is to see the difference between what I try to tell you and what you tell me."

45

Nervous laughter.

"Occasionally a project comes my way which shows a touch of genius in its flights of fancy. One such is in our hands at this moment, from Mr Bowden, of all people."

The twenty-four other people in the class suddenly realized the heat was off them, and now it was funny.

"I must say that here and there Bowden has weakened so far as to include one or two items of information that might possibly be traced to me, but generally we can say that danger is far away. Mostly we have Bowden, fair and fancy-free. Now you may know (or you may not) that a notable part of the Third Crusade was the siege of Acre by the Crusaders, after the Saracens captured it in 1187."

Tweedy held up Alec's folder and carefully opened it.

"There is a strange aroma about this document. Perhaps the author buried it to give it an historical flavour."

Tweedy was doing well. Alec sank further back in his seat. If he could sink through the floor he would have been happier.

"Ha, hm," said Tweedy and began to read.

" 'When the galleys of the barbarians had broken through our ships, our Lord Sultan Salah ad-Din Yusuf, hammer of the infidel, called to him the amirs, and took counsel with them.

" 'His nephew, the bold warrior Taki, declared that the armies of the faithful should charge down upon the besiegers and sweep them into the sea. But his brother, the wise and wily Al-Adil, counselled caution. Only wait, said he, and the Frankish bandits would fall to quarrelling among themselves like the robbers they were.' "

Tweedy stopped reading and turned to the class. Some had started to laugh; others waited to see which way the cat would jump.

"And who, Mr Bowden," asked Tweedy, "was the chief of these Frankish bandits who quarrelled among themselves over the loot?"

Without thinking, Alec said, "King Richard."

"Not the same one we all used to know of as 'The Lion Hearted'," said Tweedy. "Aha, a completely new version of history. Fascinating." He bent over the desk. "And might I know from what source you obtained this picture?"

A sinking feeling gripped Alec's stomach. He couldn't very well say that a genie in a beer can told him.

"I – I can't remember, sir."

"I wish you would try, just to satisfy my curiosity. But now that you have started on your career of rewriting history, what next may we expect? My brilliant success at blowing up the House of Commons, by Guy Fawkes; my victory over Wellington at Waterloo, by Napoleon. Ah, the mind boggles, Bowden, it boggles."

But at last Tweedy decided that he had got all the meat he could off that bone and called for silence. He began to write on the board and the rest of the lesson was spent in copying. Alec concentrated on this, but inwardly he was fuming, he was smoking, he was ready to burst into flame.

He was still running a temperature at the end of school and he slammed his books together and left the yard at twice the speed of sound. He was so aerated that he completely forgot that he had planned today to go home the long and safe way by Station Road.

He was thundering down Boner's Street before he realized what he was doing. He had reached the end of the street, near the arches, when he heard a yell:

"Bowden! I'm going to get you. Like I promised."

6

Do-it-yourself, Baghdad Style

As Ginger and his mates came charging down Boner's Street, Alec did not wait to see who was where. He made a beeline for the railway arch and looked frantically for the fourteenth plank from the right.

"There he is, under the arch," shouted Ginger. "He's mine."

Slinging his school bag round his neck and regretting bitterly for the 646th time that day that he'd forgotten his magic can, Alec desperately shoved at the loose board. He squeezed through the opening like a crash-diving worm when the early bird arrives, and sprawled among the weeds of the Tank on the other side of the fence. More shouts and the loose board behind him bulged, as Ginger and his friends pushed at it.

But Alec had recovered his wits. He didn't really believe that beefy Wallace could get through that gap, but one of Ginger's friends might be more undernourished and able to slip inside. Or they might manage to force the board back a few inches more.

"Come on, Bowden. We know you're there

behind that fence. Surrender and be destroyed. We warned you," shouted Ginger.

Alec saved his breath and made no reply. He had spotted a large lump of brickwork, part of a collapsed wall, lying among the weeds. He gave it a quick, test heave. It shifted unwillingly. Another heave and he had it on the move. It lurched on to his foot and he bit his tongue in pain.

"Give up and come out, Bowden." Ginger's voice was almost reasonable now. Aha, thought Alec, they can't get in. Then he heard a crunching sound as someone got to work on the planks with a size nine boot. He took a deep breath and heaved again at his lump of brickwork. How would Abu Salem do it? He'd just wish it over to the fence. So Alec wished and heaved and heaved and wished, and before you could say super-gravitational force fields, he had landed it with a thump against the bulging plank. There was a satisfying curse from someone who had pulled back their fingers too late. The way was blocked.

"Ah, come on, Ginger. We can get him at school tomorrow."

Alec picked up his school bag and headed across the Tank towards the canal. Another five minutes passed while he found a new piece of planking to repair his bridge after yesterday's disaster, and then he was over the canal and heading for home. He was climbing the slope above the allotments when he heard his father's train come along the viaduct.

Mum was still out shopping, but on the kitchen

table was a note asking Alec to put the kettle on and to look in the pantry. On a shelf inside the door was a newly baked treacle parkin. He cut himself a fat slice and was just sinking his teeth into it, when Dad and Mum arrived home together.

Alec could see by his mum's silence that something was up. His mother's lips were drawn together and there were none of the usual helpful remarks about his personal appearance. Dad, who was busy pouring hot water into the teapot, said nothing either. But Dad never said a lot.

As soon as Mum started to speak, Alec remembered.

"Alec love, I'm sorry, but in a week or two you'll have to move up into the boxroom and put your things in the shed."

Alec screwed his face up. He knew it was useless but he made his protest anyway.

"Aw, Mum. Why?"

"Tom, Elaine and the baby have had to get out of their rooms and they'll have to move in with us for a while again."

"Well, why should it always be me? Why can't Kim go in the boxroom?"

"OUR ALEC!" Mum always spoke in capital letters when she was annoyed. "Kim's older than you are, and she's working for her living."

"Well, I can't help it if I'm not working."

"No, I know you can't, but you might try and be a bit less expensive. That's the second pair of trainers you've ruined in twelve months."

Oh, no. Mum had spotted the trainers already.

"I'm buying a new pair myself."

"What with, eh?"

"I was thinking of borrowing some dosh from our Kim."

"You'll be lucky."

The back door banged as Kim came in, pulling her scarf from her head and kicking her outside shoes off into a corner.

"Do you have to come in like that?" asked Mum.

There were all the signs of a family row. Dad took his cup of tea and silently moved into the front room. Alec slid out of the kitchen into the passage. Then he remembered the can and rushed upstairs three at a time. He'd discovered only last week that he could do this, and it made him feel seven feet tall. Inside his own room, he dived for the bed, whipped back the pillow and . . .

IT WAS GONE.

He scurried round the room like an ant on removal day. Cupboard – no, desk – no, box – no. No, no, NO CAN. He flew to the door, flinging it open. Then he stopped and walked downstairs as casually as he could. The kitchen was quiet. Mum, Kim and Dad were sitting round eating as if nothing had happened.

"Come and have your tea, Alec," said Mum. "It's kippers. You like them and you can have another piece of parkin afterwards."

"Mum?"

"Yes?"

"Where's my can?"

"Your what, lad?"

"My beer can."

"DO YOU MEAN that smelly thing that was stuck under your pillow this morning?"

Kim shrieked with laughter.

"The lad's reverting. He'll be asking for his dummy back, soon."

"No one asked for your opinion," said Alec crushingly.

"No one ever does," snorted Kim, "but, being generous, I always give it."

Alec ignored his sister and turned again to Mum.

"Mum, seriously, where is that can?"

"Seriously, my lad, I took it and put it where it belonged, in the ash bin."

"OH NO!" spluttered Alec through his first mouthful of kippers. He stood up, kicking back his chair.

"You sit down and finish your tea."

"But . . ."

"Can I not have my tea in peace?" said Dad. Alec sat down.

"Have the dustbin men been today?"

"They're due, but I think there's a strike on at the depot. There always seems to be trouble down there these days."

Kim grunted, "If I were a dustman, I'd go on strike for ever."

"If you were a dustman, you could make a start on that room of yours," retorted her mother.

"Can I get down?" asked Alec, pushing in the last mouthful of kipper.

Hardly waiting for his mother's reply, he barged

out of the kitchen door and into the back yard. There was no sign of life from the caravan, which meant Grandad was probably down at the senior citizens' club, rolling them in the aisles with his impersonations of George Formby including some words George Formby never used.

The overflowing dustbin stood in the corner of the yard, and by it stood a pile of cans and bottles covered with an old mat. Alec leapt at the pile and threw the mat aside. Beans, custard, fruit salad. Ah, there it was. Alec picked up the familiar shiny can and looked inside, jerking back as he came face to face with a large earwig. He tipped out the insect, which was very reluctant to leave its new luxury home, and rushed indoors again.

"You're not taking that filthy thing upstairs," said Mum.

"Oh, Mum."

"Well, at least wash it out, then. It's been standing in the yard."

"I mustn't wash it."

"What do you mean, lad?" Mum took the can from him and marched over to the sink. She shot a stream of detergent through the hole in the top, followed it with a stream of hot water and shook it vigorously. Only after two changes of water, hot and cold, and a brisk rub with a tea-towel was the tin handed back, and Alec, rigid with alarm, was allowed to take it upstairs. He sank down on the bed and said breathlessly. "Salaam Aleikum, O Abu Salem."

"Aleikum Salaam, O Alec."

Alec breathed a sigh of relief. "You're all right, then?"

The genie laughed. "The renowned Shahrazad bathed in milk for the sake of her beauty, but never was there such a refreshing bath as mine. Whence came that mighty wave of foam?"

"Oh, that was detergent. But you are OK then, Abu?"

"IlHamdulilaah, thanks be to Allah. I am, as you say, OK. What is thy will?"

"Abu, I really needed you today." And Alec told the genie of the day's disasters from the time he had left home in the morning without the can, until he had rescued it from the dustbin that evening. Abu heard it all in high good humour (which rather irritated Alec), until Alec described the history lesson and Tweedy Harris's sarcasm over Alec's version of the Crusades.

"By the Beard of the Prophet. If the great and wise Ibn Khaldun knew the truth of it, why should this miserable worm say different? Say the word and his head shall never see his shoulders again. Nay, better still, we shall smite him with the Great Itch, that he may never sit down again until he has seen the truth."

Alec collapsed at the thought of Tweedy Harris smitten with the Great Itch, but he told Abu, "Oh, I think I'll let Tweedy Harris live his horrible life in peace. I've got a much more important piece of instant magic for you to perform."

"Say but the word."

55

"Not so fast, Abu. What I want you to do has to wait until dark. Meanwhile, what about a quick shish kebab? Not a feast, but a bit with bread to take away, while I do my English homework."

"Homework?"

Alec explained as simply as he could. "I have to write my own version of this story we were reading in English today."

"Ah, a merry tale?"

"Not really. It's a very modern story, about a girl who's going to have a baby and goes to live on her own."

"Aieee, such misfortunes. Nay, Alec, I know a livelier tale than that."

"What's that?"

"How Shiraz the Fair outwitted the rich old man that would have her as his bride."

Alec chuckled. "Tell on, O Abu. But not so flipping fast, so that I can get it down."

It was a long story and between bites of shish kebab and bread it took most of the evening to write down. By the time Alec had cleared away the tell-tale crumbs and opened the window to waft out the cooking aroma, it was dark.

Mum knocked on the ceiling for Alec to go to bed.

"Now then, Abu, if you're ready," he said, when the house was quiet and all lights were out.

"Thy will is my command."

Alec told Abu the sorry story of Tom, Elaine and the baby, of the boxroom and his own gloomy future. Abu hummed and ha-ed a little. "If you

would have me make a new place for thy brother
and his family, I fear that may take time."

"Don't be daft, Abu. All I want is for you to
make an extension to the house."

"Extension?"

"Oh, Abu, didn't they ever have do-it-yourself at
the court of Haroun Al Raschid?"

"Why, Alec, who would do-it-himself when there
were slaves to command?"

"I see your point, Abu."

So Alec tried to explain with diagrams and much
pointing out of the window into the back yard, what
he wanted. At last Abu said, "It is well; it shall be
done. Now I must depart for a while. Ma'asalaama."

"Ma'aslaama, Abu."

There was silence for several minutes. Through
the window Alec could see the familiar shape of the
railway arch in the night sky.

Suddenly the wall of his room began to tremble.
Then it glowed with a strange green light and began
to fade away until it had vanished completely, and
all that was left was a dark emptiness.

"Hey, Abu. What are you playing at?"

"One moment, O Alec . . ." The genie sounded
breathless.

Out of the dark emptiness came a shape, first of
walls and then of a floor extending into the night.
Again there was a strange glow, but this gradually
merged with the light of the room. Now the room
stretched away in front of him. It seemed to be
yards long and it was covered wall-to-wall with a
luxurious, deep blue carpet; on either side were

couches, chairs, and a soft-looking bed under a silk canopy. At the end of the room a big window opened to the sky. Abu had done him proud; it was a do-it-yourself extension palace and no mistake.

He sprang off the bed and ran barefoot into the new room. He sank his feet into the soft carpet and threw himself down on the floor, rolled around, then leapt up on the bed and bounced on it like a trampoline. He didn't know where to sit next, it all seemed so comfortable. Last of all he raced to the big window and looked out to see how far the extension reached.

As he did, there came a strange noise.

Someone was calling, "Help! Help!"

He looked down into the yard and he gave a horrified shout.

"Abu, come back! Salaam Aleikum . . as quick as you can."

"Help! help! help! . . ."

All was dark at the back of the house, but Alec could vaguely see what had happened. Abu's do-it-yourself king-size extension had filled the back yard completely and there wasn't room for the caravan any more. It had been thrown on its side, with one wheel whirling madly away. From the window Granddad's white head poked out with his hair blowing in the night breeze, while he shouted for help.

"Abuuuu!" yelled Alec.

"What is thy will, O Alec?" The genie was completely out of breath.

"Quick! We've caused a catastrophe here. Get

this extension out of the way and put the caravan right way up again."

"But this palace was made only at the cost of much effort."

"Well, you'd better make some more effort and do away with it. Granddad is going daft in there."

"Thy will is my command," said Abu, but he sounded very peeved. There was a rushing sound, a creaking and crumbling and the magnificent room, its furnishings, its lights and its great window vanished so suddenly that Alec seemed to be left floating on air. Then he dropped with a bump that shook the sense out of him. He looked wildly round. He was standing in his pyjamas by the caravan, which was now back in its place. The door opened and Granddad stood on the steps in his nightshirt and flashed a little torch.

"Hey up, Alec. What are you doing, lad? You'll catch your death. Come in here."

Granddad stretched out his hand and hauled Alec inside. Then he fiddled about lighting a little lamp by his bunk.

"Hey, lad. It looks as though we've both had nightmares. You wandering about in your pyjamas and me dreaming the caravan was tipped over and I was shouting for help."

"Oh, you were shouting for help, Granddad. That's why I . . ." Alec stopped. How could he possibly explain even to Granddad just what had happened?

"It's a wonder we didn't wake up the whole street between us, then," said Granddad. He peered out of the window. "Well, your mum and dad didn't hear anything. Mind you, with them sleeping in the front bedroom, they wouldn't anyway." He ruffled Alec's hair.

"Well, I never made you out for a sleepwalker, Alec." He paused. "I reckon you'd best stay here. If you go back now, they'll hear you and then there'll be no end of argument. Look, lad, you get up on my bed and I'll sit in the old armchair. Now don't fuss, I'm quite comfortable. Up you get."

Alec climbed up and lay down on the bunk. The bedclothes were still warm and he soon felt drowsy. Granddad pulled a blanket over him and, putting out the bedside lamp, sat down in his chair. As Alec's eyes became used to the dark, he could just see the old man's face.

"Granddad?"

"What is it?"

"Tell us something."

The old man chuckled, shifted in his chair and cleared his throat.

> " 'Twas Christmas Day in the workhouse
> And the snow was raining fast
> And a barefooted lad with clogs on
> Stood sitting in the grass . . ."

Granddad's voice grew slowly fainter.

> "The bees were making beeswax
> And the skies were dark and clear
> 'Twas a June day in December,
> In the middle of next year . . ."

Alec was asleep.

7

High Noon at Bugletown Comprehensive

Alec was late to school next day. By the time he had finished explaining to Mum how he came to be sleeping in the caravan, it was gone nine o'clock. He missed Registration and Assembly, but he caught Miss Welch in one of the corridors, gave her his homework and managed to make his excuses to Mr Foster, his form teacher.

"All right, Alec, but get a grip on yourself, laddie. I don't think you're quite with us these days. People are beginning to talk about you. I hear whispers from the English Department and the History Department that you're going funny in your old age."

That was a laugh. Mr Foster who taught Religious Instruction was as old as the hills and well known for his faraway look. The story went that he tied a piece of wool round one finger to remind him to come to school and another piece round the next finger to remind him what the first piece was for! But he shook his head at Alec in a friendly way and sent him off to maths in good spirits. Alec had other reasons for good cheer. First, by coming late he had missed Ginger Wallace and Co.; second, he had remembered to put his can in his jacket pocket when he got dressed. So far, so good, Bowden. Disasters one, triumphs nil, but there was still a chance to equalize before half time.

His chance came in English just before lunch. Miss Welch walked round the class giving out exercise books. As she handed Alec's back, she stopped.

"Well, Alec, I enjoyed your story. It wasn't much to do with *The L-Shaped Room*, but it was funnier."

Alec's head began to swell slightly.

"I liked the part where Shiraz the Fair left the old man sitting up the palm tree in his nightshirt. But did you make it up yourself?"

Alec was ready for that one. "Oh, no, Miss, I sort of adapted it from *The Arabian Nights*."

"Funny, I had a quick look through this morning and I couldn't spot any story like it. Ah, well, a stroke of natural genius, I suppose." Miss Welch went on her way.

Genius. She didn't know how true it was, thought Alec, as he made the score in his head, disasters one, triumphs one. Just then the pips went for lunch break. He packed away his books and, without a care in the world, shot out into the schoolyard.

Right into the arms (well, not quite, but near enough) of Ginger Wallace and three of his friends from Boner's Street. Alec looked madly from side to side, but there was no escape. The duty master was out of sight, as usual, and there wasn't a sign of anyone from 3F who might stand by him.

"Right, Bowden, say your prayers, man." It was clear that Ginger was a keen Western fan.

"I don't know what you're talking about, Ginger," said Alec as calmly and amiably as he could.

"Mr Wallace to you. You're not allowed the honour of calling me Ginger. You were down Boner's Street last night, after I told you you weren't coming down there any more. Right? If you hadn't slipped into the woodwork, we'd have got you then. We don't like to make a mess in the schoolyard, but it can't be helped."

For a second Alec thought of buying off Ginger by letting him into the secret of the Tank, but then he thought he wouldn't. He was going to keep that secret whatever . . . ooh, he saw Ginger's fist double up, big and brown.

"Hey, what's this?"

Alec looked round him. Behind him were Sam Taylor and two of his mates. Alec disliked Sam Taylor. He was a bully, and as thick as two planks, as well as being spotty, but right now he could have kissed him! Well, almost.

Ginger snorted.

"What do you want, Taylor? Want me to knock some spots off for you?"

Ginger's mates laughed, but not very loudly.

"Very funny, Mohammad Ali. You've got a big mouth, just like him."

"What do you want, Spotty?" Ginger refused to be diverted.

Taylor became pompous. "You think you're going to bash one of our lads, don't you, Wallace? Well, you're not."

"What do you mean, 'our lads'? Skinny's in 3F, not 3D."

"You know what I mean, Wallace, I mean our lads."

Taylor raised his voice and Alec saw why. Others from Spotty's form were gathering round, neutral, but interested. Suddenly Ginger and his mates seemed rather thin on the ground. There weren't more than twenty or thirty black kids in the school altogether. Alec could see why Ginger had to be cock of the walk in Boner's Street.

"OK, Wallace. What are you going to do? Apologize to Skinny?"

Ginger's face hardened.

"You can get . . ." and he moved forward, both fists up.

"Hey, wait a minute," said one of Taylor's mates. "If Cartwright catches us now, we'll be for the high jump. Let's sort it out outside school tonight."

"What, and have the law on to us? No, let's have it now."

"Tell you what," Taylor's mate had an inspiration, "let's have a game of backers up by the railings. If we win, Wallace says sorry to Skinny. If they win, we forget it."

Spotty and Ginger looked doubtful, but their friends shouted, "Yes, backers, backers!"

"OK," said Taylor grudgingly. "How many a side? You'll have problems raising a team, won't you?"

Ginger clenched his teeth. "You worry about

yourselves. We'll play six a side, but I'll tell you one thing. You've got to play Bowden on your side."

"Skinny? Get off with you," said Taylor.

"Oh, what's the sweat?" said his friends. "We can leather them any road. Come on before someone comes and breaks it up." By now a crowd had gathered, some of the senior boys hovering discreetly in the background. Taylor waved his arm in a wide sweep and led the team he had chosen to the railings, followed by Ginger and his chosen five. A spin of the coin and Taylor lost.

"OK, Wallace," he grunted to Ginger. "Your mob bats first."

Ginger and the others lined up, their number one man taking a firm grip on the iron railings, then bending down. Number two grasped the first man's hips and bent down likewise until all six were lined up, crocodile fashion. Alec noticed that Ginger took the middle position, where most of the weight would fall. He admired him for that.

"Go!" shouted Spotty Sam and the game began.

As Ginger had foreseen, most of the weight fell on him. Alec, who was last to jump, landed towards the back of the line. His team-mates were in a clutching heap further along.

Ginger's team started to count. "One, two, three . . ." The noise from the crowd became deafening as the count went on. But ten came with Ginger's men still holding tight. Sam's team piled off, looking grim.

"Right," said their leader. "If we hold you lot this time we'll play two more goes. OK?"

"Many as you like," said Ginger jauntily and led his men out.

"OK, get fell in," ordered Sam. "Charlie, you take the railings. Skinny, you can go number two. They won't be able to reach you there. All you have to do is hold on to Charlie. Get down. Hey, where are you lot going?" he demanded of Ginger as Ginger's team withdrew to the other side of the yard.

"Just getting a good run up, that's all."

Alec, bent double, clutching Charlie's hips, looked back through his own legs. Ginger's men had backed right off to the wall that stood between the girls' and boys' yards. Above the wall could be seen the heads of girls who had climbed up to see the fun. Alec could see the broad, handsome face of Ginger's sister, but she was not smiling. Around them in the yard a huge crowd had gathered. Alec could see no teachers but they must have their eyes on this by now.

"OK, go!" shouted Ginger. Alec took a last look as Ginger's closest friend, a tall, thin boy, began his run up. Alec heard the beat of the footsteps coming nearer; suddenly they stopped. A second more and he felt a terrific thump in the small of his back. Spotty Sam had underestimated the other team. Their first man had made a fantastic leap and Alec got the full weight. He began to sweat and he felt his hands slipping.

"Hold on, Skinny, for Pete's sake," muttered Charlie.

The second man began his run. He landed well forward, so did the third man, but the fourth and fifth who were smaller boys landed further back. After the fifth there was a pause. The last man, Alec knew, must be Ginger. Why was he waiting? The weight of the lad on top of him was bearing down in the small of his back. Alec began to feel sick and dizzy. He tried to hook his fingers into Charlie's pocket. He mustn't let go, but how long could he hold on?

Sam Taylor yelled, "Come on, Wallace. Stop mucking about. If you can't jump, give in."

Ginger ignored him. Instead he shouted to his team mates, "Down, all of you. Down."

The run up began. Alec heard in a daze the crunch of Ginger's boots. The school yard was silent. The sweat ran down Alec's nose and dripped off in a stream. Ginger jumped and Alec almost passed out as the weight on him suddenly doubled. Ginger had leapt so far forward that he was on top of his team mate and both of them were on top of Alec. His fingers began to slip. Desperately he let go with one hand.

"They're giving," yelled Ginger.

Alec twisted his arm inside his jacket, strained an inch or two and touched the can.

"Salaam Aleikum. Give me strength."

He felt a great rush of power. He arched his back. The weight suddenly vanished. They'd fallen off. He stood upright. He looked round. There was the sound of cheering. Ginger's team lay sprawled on the ground, all except Ginger, who was perched on the railings and looked dazed.

Sam Taylor crowed like a rooster. "That's fixed 'em," he yelled. Ginger leapt off the fence with fury in his eyes. "You lot cheated. You shifted. You humped us off. You can't even play your own game fairly!"

He hurled himself at Sam Taylor and punching and kicking the two rolled over on to the ground. In a second Ginger's team-mates were on their feet, wading into the rest of Sam's team. Alec, his strength suddenly departed, received a clout over the side of his head which sent him reeling to the fence with bells ringing in his ears.

The scrap became general and other kids joined in. Ginger's team were getting a pounding. Alec stared in amazement as over the wall swarmed Ginger's sister and her friends, screaming like furies. From the corner of his eye, Alec saw her with Charlie's flowing locks firmly gripped in one hand, while she battered his nose with the other. It must have been agony.

The inevitable happened.

"Break it up, break it up. Taylor! Wallace!"

Mr Cartwright and the duty teacher, Mr Evans the games master, were rushing across the yard, grabbing at collars and arms, pulling warriors apart. Miss Bentley was there too. She had two girls in what looked like a judo grip. That must have been painful too. Alec felt himself grabbed. Mr Evans's furious face stared into his.

"You, Bowden, get out of it."

Alec felt the side of a size fifteen shoe catch him in the seat of his pants and he flew towards the school door.

Ten minutes later, the battle had been broken up

and fifteen prisoners had been taken from both sides in the game, plus three girls. They were lined up under guard in Mr Cartwright's office.

"I don't know what started this, although I shall find out. But I'll give you this warning. Any more of *this* kind of fighting in the school and someone's for the high jump. You know what I mean, don't you? Now get out."

The prisoners nodded, relieved at the mildness of their treatment and went back to their classrooms.

Later that afternoon, Alec was cross-examined by Mr Cartwright. He tried to explain what had happened and Mr Cartwright nodded. Then he said, "Just as a matter of interest, why do you go home down Boner's Street?"

Alec hesitated. "Oh, it's just a habit. I used to go down there when my mate lived in Boner's, that's all, sir."

"There's no way through to the estate from Boner's Street, surely?"

"Oh, er yes," said Alec vaguely.

"Ah, one last question. Wallace swears that you threw him on the railings. Can you explain that extraordinary feat?"

"Oh, er no."

"All right. Now look, Alec. We're going to let this matter lie. There's obviously something between you and this lad, Ginger Wallace. Just keep clear of him and don't join any line-ups like we had in the schoolyard today or there'll be big trouble. Now buzz off."

8

Make with the Shekels

Friday teatime was always a favourite of Alec's. There was usually something special, and this week Kim had brought home cream cakes from work. With the weekend round the corner everyone was in a good mood. Dad, who was on the early turn and had slept a little in the afternoon, was in a quiet good humour and Granddad had been persuaded to come in from the caravan and have tea with the rest of the family. All was quiet and peaceful save for the tap of knife on plate or spoon on saucer.

Then Dad, who had finished his tea and had picked up the *Bugletown Gazette* to read, dropped a bombshell.

"I see our family's been in the wars."

"What do you mean, Harold?" said Mum.

Dad eased his spectacles on his nose and began to read slowly.

" 'Poltergeists in Bugletown?' – that's the headline, with a question mark."

"Go on, our Dad," said Kim, impatiently.

" 'Ghosts and other strange things that go bump in the night are usually associated with stately homes, but it seems Bugletown's pre-war council estate at Roundhill has acquired a ghost or poltergeist. Senior citizen Harry Bowden, who retired five years ago, after fifty years' service with the railways, told our reporter of an alarming experience which occurred during Wednesday night.

" ' "I was just about to go to bed, when the caravan in which I sleep suffered a sudden violent shock. For a moment it seemed as though it was turned on its side, then just as suddenly it was upright again. I was tempted to imagine that I had had a bad dream, but it all seemed so real, and bear in mind, I had not yet got into bed."

" 'Mr Archibald Forrester, chairman of the Bugletown Society for the Investigation of Psychic Phenomena, who had questioned Mr Bowden closely . . .' "

"I bet he did," interrupted Kim, "in the saloon bar at the Three Fiddlers. Spirit research all right!"

Granddad looked pained. Dad went on reading:

" '. . . closely, is of the opinion that psychic forces, perhaps from prehistoric times, when Round Hill is reputed to have been the scene of ancient rites, are at work. He has asked Mr Bowden and any other Bugletown citizens to report to him any similar incidents.' "

Kim burst into laughter; Dad smiled a bit; Alec was torn between laughter and the thought that it might hurt Granddad, plus the thought that he was really to blame himself for the incident. But suddenly Mum spoke angrily.

"GRANDDAD! I wonder you haven't got more sense."

"What do you mean?" said Granddad. "I only told the *Gazette* reporter what happened."

"Hasn't it occurred to you that, thanks to that story, it'll be all over town that you're living in that caravan? And noseyparker Councillor Blaggett from the Housing Committee will be round because one of his regulations has been broken? And you know what that'll mean?"

Granddad was silent.

"You're supposed to be living in the house with us, otherwise the council will start wanting you to go into the old people's home on the other side of town. I suppose you'd like that."

Granddad looked miserable.

"Oh, Mother, don't go on so," said Kim. "Councillor Blaggett won't find out. He only reads the paper to find out if there's anything there about himself."

"It's all right for you, our Kim, but I'm the one who has to do the worrying round here," said Mum, shooting a glance at Dad, who had gone back to reading the *Gazette*.

"Hey," said Dad a moment later, "I wasn't joking when I said our family had been in the wars. There's our Alec's school here as well."

"What does it say?"

"Listen to it: 'Race riot at Bugletown Comprehensive'. That's the headline . . ."

"Race riot? Get off – never," exploded Kim. "What'll they think of next? Why, there's hardly any black people round here."

"There's a lot in Boner's Street," said Mum. "Miss Morris is always going on about them. She has a family living upstairs from her. She reckons they put coal in the bath."

Granddad suddenly choked on his cream cake.

"Hetty Morris wouldn't know what a bath's for."

"That's very unkind, Granddad."

"Well, I sat next to her at the Senior Citizens' Club yesterday and I ought to know." Granddad wrinkled his nose.

"She reckons they ought to re-house them out at Moorside. Some of those houses in Boner's Street are real slums."

"Would Hetty Morris go and live out at Moorside?" demanded Granddad. "You bet your life she wouldn't. And those houses in Boner's Street are a long way from being slums. They're overcrowded, but the buildings are in better shape than some of the houses on this estate. They only need seeing to."

Alec took deep breath.

"Anyway, it's a lot of old toffee. There wasn't a riot at our school. It was just a punch-up, black against white."

"And how do you know so well?"

"Because I was in it. There was Ginger Wallace and his mates from Boner's Street on one side, and Spotty Sam, I mean Sam Taylor, and his mates on the other."

"What were you doing in it?"

"Well, er, I . . ."

Dad put his paper on one side. "Perhaps Alec should go up and get his homework out of the way for the weekend. I'm off to the Club for my meeting." He rose. Mum looked displeased but said nothing. Alec and Kim began to clear the table and Granddad went quietly out of the back door.

"Did you say Wallace?" Kim asked Alec.

He nodded.

"I think I know his mother. She works on our section at the factory. She's all right. Her daughter goes to your school, a smashing looking girl called Eulalia."

"Eulalia?"

"That's right. Do you know her, Alec?" Kim suddenly looked across the table and Alec blushed.

"What are you blushing for? Hey, Mum, our Alec's blushing."

"Gerroff," growled Alec.

"He's growing up, you know. He's started noticing the other sex."

"Shut up, will you?" said Alec.

"Stop it, you two! Leave those tea things and get out of here. You make my head ache with your rowing."

Alec went upstairs. His homework was done in under an hour. There was plenty of light. But he felt fed up with everything.

All that argument at the tea table had spoilt the Friday evening feeling. Why did people have to row about everything? Why did Mum have to worry about Councillor Blaggett nosing round? He changed into his jumper and jeans and wandered out to the back. Granddad was sitting on the caravan steps looking glum.

"Is it right, Granddad, what Mum said about Councillor Blaggett? Could he make trouble for you?"

"Well, he could and all. I'm supposed to be living

74

in the house, not in the caravan. Your dad's only supposed to use that for holidays."

"Well, never mind, Granddad. If he comes round, you can have my room, and I'll go in the boxroom."

Granddad ruffled Alec's hair.

"You're a good lad, Alec. But you're forgetting that our Tom, Elaine and the baby are moving back in as well. If I were you, I'd keep that under your hat, too. If some helpful person reported that to the council, there'd be trouble."

"But couldn't Tom and Elaine get a flat in one of those blocks out at Moorside?"

"They might. Now Moorside's a lovely place. Well, it was anyway. But it's best for peewits and skylarks, not for people. One pub and two shops, no place for the kids and four miles out from Penfold, let alone six miles from Bugletown. It gets parky there in winter, I can tell you."

Alec was silent for a moment, then,

"Granddad. Do you reckon it's right, what Miss Morris said about the Wallaces keeping coal in the bath?"

Granddad chuckled.

"How should I know? I've never been in the Wallaces' and I'll bet Hetty Morris never did. But I'll tell you something for nothing. When we first moved into these council houses before the war, the people down in Boner's Street used to say we kept coal in the bath. It's an old sort of joke, if you can call it a joke.

"Gracie Fields used to sing a song, you know . . .

" *'We'll have a bathroom, a beeyootiful bathroom And a lovely bath where we can keep the coal . . .'* "

75

Granddad sang so loudly that Alec felt embarrassed and looked round to see if anyone was listening. Granddad stopped singing just as suddenly as he started and burst into laughter.

"People in Boner's Street were very posh in those days. When I was a lad, we lived in Upshaw Street, off School Lane. When kids from Boner's Street came down our way, going to the grammar school, that's where your school is now, we used to make them go the long way round. We used to give them a right pasting if they didn't."

Granddad looked at Alec's amazed expression.

"Why, what's up, lad? Have I said anything wrong?"

"Oh no, Granddad. You just made me think of something, that's all."

Next day, Alec was allowed to stay in bed as long as he liked. But he felt restless and got up to moon around the kitchen until his mother sent him out to Station Road, to pick up something she had forgotten when she and Dad did the shopping on Friday. Alec suddenly had an idea.

He raced upstairs, took the can from beneath his pillow and woke up Abu.

"Salaam Aleikum, Abu. Keef Haalak? How are you this bright and sunny morning?"

"IlHamdulilaah," responded Abu sleepily. "What is thy wish?"

"We're going shopping. I need some money. So make with the shekels."

"How much is it your wish that I should make?"

"Oh, fifty pence, I reckon."

76

"What is fifty pence?"

"Oh, Abu, surely a genius like you ought to know that. It's a seven-sided silvery coin about this big." Alec held out his hand. In that instant a coin appeared in it. He thrust it into his pocket, ushered Abu back into the can and went out. He kept his own shopping until last. He had his eye on a rather special sort of ice-cream with fruit, nuts and a dash of something or other like rum. It usually cost too much, but not today, ah, not today. He breezed into the shop and slapped the coin on the counter. The shopkeeper looked at it, turned it over and grinned.

"Look, Alec. I know we're part of the EEC and all, but this won't do. Why, it's not even European. It looks as though it came from the Middle East or somewhere."

He turned away to serve a young man who had just come in asking for cigarettes, leaving Alec staring at the coin with its intricate network of Arabic lettering. He might have known. He just might have known. There had to be a snag somewhere.

"Let's have a look at that, kid."

Alec looked up. The young man, tall, slightly pimply and dark haired, stood over him, holding out his hand. Alec held up the coin, but was reluctant to let it go. The young man's eyes narrowed.

"That's a nice coin." He gestured with his shoulder and Alec followed him out of the shop. "I collect coins like this. I'll give you – hm – twenty-five pence for it."

Alec hesitated. It wasn't much, but then, if he wanted English money –

"Fifty pence," he said impulsively.

"All right, I'll give you thirty pence for it. Where did you get it?"

Alec shrugged, pocketing the thirty pence.

"Got any more like it? I'm interested," wheedled the young man.

"I might have one or two."

"Tell you what. You get me some more and I'll give you a quid for every four. How's that?"

"I'll think about it."

"Look. I'll meet you at the bottom of the station steps at two o'clock tomorrow. I'll have up to five quid on me. It's up to you, kid."

Alec went home slowly and thoughtfully. Once home he climbed up to his bedroom and took out the can. He explained to Abu what he wanted. Abu was silent for a moment.

"I like it not, O Alec."

"Yours not to reason why, Abu. Make with the shekels."

Abu made disapproving noises but produced twenty shining coins of the same shape and size. Alec opened his drawer where he kept odds and ends, old badges, tokens, marbles, and took out a bag to put the coins in. Then he put it in his back pocket.

That afternoon it rained and he passed the time in his room with Abu, having a quiet feast and talking of this and that. Abu told him of the great scientists and astronomers of his day. Alec told him of the great modern inventions, the jet plane, the motor car, space travel and television.

"It is all as written in the Great Book of Magic," said Abu, "the magic carpet, the all-seeing mirror, the flying horse. Yet from all you have told me, man is no happier."

"Oh, you're just an old pessimist, Abu," said Alec. He'd begun to feel a little uneasy about the genie. The more he knew him, the more he liked him. He was great company, but he had developed a rather nasty habit of commenting on things and giving advice, even when it wasn't asked.

On Sunday, when he went to meet the young man outside Bugletown Railway Station, he left Abu under the pillow. He handed over the bag and received in exchange five, highly useful, pound coins. On the whole he felt pleased with the weekend. He reckoned triumphs one, disasters nil, the first win for the home team this season.

That evening, though, before he went to bed, he had a sudden disturbing thought. Ginger Wallace must still be brooding over last week's defeat. He might do nothing at school, but on the other hand he might well lay an ambush in Boner's Street. Alec had no intention of changing his route home from school. He was going to go home through Boner's Street and the Tank, and Ginger Wallace should not be allowed to interfere with that.

He called up Abu for the last time that day and placed the problem before him. Abu pondered for a moment, then said,

"Rest assured, O Alec, sleep in peace. Tomorrow thy troubles will vanish like snow in the desert."

9

Abu In High Spirits

School was quiet and peaceful that week. There was no sign of Ginger Wallace; it seemed his mother had kept him home. For the first day or two Spotty Sam went about boasting that Wallace couldn't take it, but after a while no one thought it was funny.

Alec felt distinctly triumphal with five pound coins in his back pocket and his trusty can in his inside pocket. He bought himself a new pair of trainers, and though his mother might have been a bit suspicious, she wasn't complaining. He found a copy of *Treasure Island* in the second-hand paperback shop and bought that. But, otherwise, like Biggs after the Great Train Robbery, he lay low and kept off the big spending. He didn't want awkward questions about the source of his wealth. Apart from which he had a sneaking feeling that he hadn't got Abu the Instant Genie programmed right yet. There was an art to this magic can business.

Eulalia Wallace was at school, but looking grim. She passed Alec without laughing or making a face and this rather irritated him, though he tried not to show it. In the schoolyard at break times the soldiery figure of Monty Cartwright was to be seen, keeping an eye on things. Quarrels and grudges tended to fade and people passed the time in proving games of poker and brag in quiet corners. Life was so quiet that, by the middle of the week, Alec was beginning to be a trifle bored.

On Thursday it rained and at lunchtime Alec felt he should pay an overdue visit to the club which Mr Jameson ran in the science laboratory. As he drifted in, a small group of second years were watching the installation of new pair of hamsters in one of the cages. The last pair were rumoured to be roaming the central heating pipes, coming out at night to feed off samples of homework books.

There was a weird smell about the place. At least there was a new weird smell. Alec's nose traced it to the back of the lab where three sixth-formers were busy with a complicated apparatus of tubes and retorts, all hissing and bubbling. Mr Jameson greeted him like a long-lost friend. A little too hearty, Alec thought, as though he'd been in the Antarctic for several years. But he didn't mind. Mr Jameson's mickey-taking was different somehow from Tweedy Harris's sarcasm.

Half an hour passed pleasantly and the other kids were drifting away. Alec took his chance to get Mr Jameson on his own and asked him,

"Sir, is it possible to make things materialize and dematerialize?" He had to struggle with the last word, but Mr Jameson waited.

"Well, matter can change from solid to liquid,

liquid to gas can't it? And if the gas is colourless, you could say it disappears, but it's still there in another form."

"No, sir, I wasn't thinking about that. I was thinking, like, say," Alec paused for a moment, "the story about Aladdin's lamp and the genie who made money appear and lifted up palaces and shot them across the world."

"Hm. Well, I suppose our space rockets are just as fantastic. When a rocket lands it comes so quickly it appears out of nowhere. They say that one of the worst things about the V-2 rockets during the Second World War was that they just landed, without warning."

"But, sir. Do you think things could be made to dematerialize somewhere and then materialize somewhere else? Like a genie does, I mean."

"Well, if you could break things down into their atoms and then reassemble them. It's a theoretical possibility, but a practical impossibility, I should have thought."

"The-o-retical?"

"I mean, you can work it out in your mind, how it might be done, but the problems involved in doing it are too great. Now the old alchemists thought you could transform lead into gold. You might be inclined to laugh at them, but that would be wrong because we know that the atomic weight of lead and gold are close to one another. In theory one could vary the structure of one so it changed into the other."

"What are we waiting for then, sir?"

Mr Jameson laughed. "Because it would cost more time, money and effort than the gold would be worth. Anyway, lead is very useful and valuable. If you worked in an atomic reactor a lead shield would be a million times more valuable than a gold one."

"But the alchemists were right?"

"Oh, yes. The man who imagined a flying horse was right and so was the man who imagined the magic mirror that could see what other people were doing."

"Oh, that's what Abu said . . ." Alec broke in excitedly.

"Abu? Who's he? Which year is he in?"

"Oh, nothing, sir." Alec was confused. "Thanks very much, sir, anyway. I've never understood things as well before."

"You've never asked such searching questions before."

Alec was about to go when he was called back by one of the sixth-formers who lived on the estate.

"Alec. D'you think your granddad would like a drop of our jungle juice?"

"Jungle juice. What's that?"

"Oh, it's just something we're brewing up here." He lowered his voice. "The powers that be are not supposed to know."

Across the lab, Alec thought he saw Mr Jameson's shoulders begin to shake.

"We'll find a bottle for you," said the sixth-former. "Wait a bit, though. Is that an empty can you've got in your pocket there?"

"Er . . .' said Alec.

"Come on, give. That's better than a bottle. We'll seal it with sticking plaster and you can take it home to the old man with our best wishes."

Not knowing how to refuse, Alec handed over his can. It was filled, sealed and handed back to him.

"Hurry up, lads, lessons start in thirty seconds flat," said Mr Jameson.

Alec left the lab. He could feel the liquid swishing in the can in his pocket. If he could nip into one of the washrooms and tip it out . . .

"That's the wrong way for English, Alec."

He looked up in dismay. Miss Welch, grinning cheerfully, stood in his path. Reluctantly he was steered into the classroom. Seated at his desk and keeping one eye on Miss Welch who was writing on the board, Alec quietly tried to scrape the sticking plaster off the top of the can.

"What *are* you doing back there, Alec?" Miss Welch was looking at him. Alec slipped the can on to the floor. Perhaps if he allowed the can to lie on its side the liquid would seep out. "Miss," squeaked Alice Rogers, "Alec Bowden's wetting the floor."

Miss Welch steamed over from the front of the room and Alec slipped the can back into his pocket. It was upside down though and he could feel the liquid slowly draining out. If Miss Welch would only look away, he could slip the can into his school bag. But the wet patch on his trousers was uncomfortable, as well as embarrassing.

Miss Welch sniffed. "Peculiar smell in this room. Like essence of burnt rubber."

She went back to the board and finished her writing.

"Right, you lot. Answer those questions. I'm out for twenty minutes. But don't get any ideas. Mr Cartwright has promised to keep his eyes on you." She went out and after the first burst of noisy whispering the class was silent, save for the occasional mutter or cough. Alec waited five minutes and then slipped out through the door. A few yards down the corridor he was stopped.

"Mr Bowden, I presume. Whither away?"

It was Monty speaking through the partly open door of his office.

"Just to the toilets, sir."

"Hm."

Alec scurried into the washroom, hastily ripped off the plaster seal and emptied the can. The liquid was a cheerful golden colour in spite of its pong.

He was sure Granddad would have liked it, but he had to think of his own interests and Abu's. When the can was empty, he slipped it back into his inside pocket and walked back to the classroom. As he entered, Mr Cartwright had been on a reconnaissance. Now all was deadly quiet, save for the mournful squeak of a pen here and there.

Suddenly there came a tremendous belch. Those nearest Alec turned round.

"Bowden, you dirty old man," said Ronnie Carter, who sat just in front of him.

"It wasn't me," said Alec, truthfully.

"Not much, it wasn't. You're disgusting."

"Oh, belt up," whispered Alec, as he heard footsteps in the corridor.

"Haa-up-errp." This time there was a combined hiccup and belch. Then Alec's heart stood still as this was followed by a sudden burst of singing in a lively, but slurred, baritone.

"Hey, give over, Bowden. You'll have Cartwright here in a minute."

"You *have* Cartwright in here!" said a voice from the doorway. "What is the excitement about?"

He was answered by a series of hiccups, fired off like a machine gun.

Then a ferocious burp and another line of the Baghdad Genies' Anthem, or whatever it was Abu was singing.

Mr Cartwright's eyes opened wide. "Bowden?" he said, with shock in his voice.

"It's my transistor," said Alec, desperately.

"Well, switch it off."

"I can't, it's stuck in my pocket. Please can I go outside, sir?"

"I'd strongly recommend it," said Mr Cartwright menacingly, "and stand outside my room. What are you laughing about?"

"I'm not laughing, sir." But the laughter, full, hearty drunken, laughter, mocked him. The sounds of singing and hiccuping followed Alec as he fled red-faced down the corridor and into the washroom. They finally disappeared in gargling and bubbling sounds as Alec turned on a tap and sent a stream of cold water pouring into the can. He emptied it, refilled and emptied it again, shook it, rubbed it against his coat, and then raised it to his ear. Only the faintest of snoring sounds could now be heard. He put the can into his pocket and went down the corridor to Mr Cartwright's office.

"Come in, come in. Shut the door."

Oh, thought Alec, that sounds nasty.

"Sit down over there."

"Ah, that sounds better," he thought.

"I'm sure I don't know what you're playing at, Alec Bowden," said Mr Cartwright. "I'm equally sure that song was never broadcast, even on Cairo Radio, even if you could get it on your transistor. May I ask where you picked it up? Have you any idea what the words meant? And why the belches and hiccups?"

Alec's mouth opened, but he couldn't think of a sensible answer to any of the questions. Mr Cartwright, however, was not looking for answers today; he steamed on.

"Your interest in things Arabian is quite remarkable. The History Department let me have a look at your Crusader project."

Alec groaned. This was disaster day, all right.

"Very interesting. I read it with some fascination. I served for years in the Middle East and I came to realize that the Arabs have quite a different view of history from ours."

"That's right, sir. They thought the Crusaders were a pack of barbarians."

Cartwright nodded. "The trouble was, their civilization was on the way down, and ours in the West was on the way up. We owe them a lot."

This time Alec stopped himself from saying, "That's what Abu says." Instead he said on impulse, "I don't see why any civilization should be up while another's down, sir. It'd be better if they were all on the same level."

Mr Cartwright nodded and laughed. "You're probably right, but it's easier said than done. Look at the problems in this school now. There's Miss Welch doing her best to teach you English and you disrupting the lesson with impersonations of a drunken Arab."

"I'm sorry, sir."

"I believe you. Thousands wouldn't. I don't think you're a troublemaker, Alec Bowden, but trouble certainly centres round you. See if you can keep out of it. Now clear off."

Alec felt cheerful on his way from school. Near disaster had been avoided. He couldn't claim a goal for triumphs, but he could reckon a goalless draw for the day. In order not to spoil his team's chances, he decided to give Boner's Street a miss and go home along Station Road.

He was cheerfully crossing the open space in front of the railway station, thinking about how he would have a quiet chat and feast with Abu after the genie had slept off his orgy that evening, when he was stopped violently in his tracks. A hand came out of nowhere, gripped his collar and nearly strangled him.

"Hey, leggo," he gasped. He jerked round and found himself face to face with the tall young man he had done the currency deal with at the weekend.

But this time the young man was not smiling. He was looking dangerous.

"You little . . . you conned me."

Alec turned white. "I never . . . You gave me five quid, I gave you twenty coins. And you got a bargain. I reckon they were worth more."

"Twenty coins? Twenty flipping milk tokens."

Alec nearly passed out as the young man waved in his face the marble bag Alec had given him. What had happened? He must have given him the wrong bag, but how . . .?

"I'm sorry. I didn't mean to con you. Look, I'll go home and get you another lot."

"You'll give me my five quid back, that's what you'll do, and quick." His collar was given an extra twist and Alec started to choke. He dropped his satchel, felt in his back pocket and produced four coins. Then, from his other pocket, he found twenty pence in loose change.

"That's all I've got left, but I'll get it for you by the weekend."

The young man's face reddened. He gave Alec's collar yet another twist.

"I want it all back, today. Right now."

"Arthur Blaggett. What do you think you're on about?" At the sound of the voice behind him, the young man let Alec go with a jerk. Alec bent, picked up his satchel and moved off sharply.

"Just a minute, Alec, where are you off to?"

It was Kim on her way home from work, raincoat over her overalls, handbag swinging from her arm, with an angry frown on her face.

"Come on, now, Alec. What's it all about?"

Reluctantly, Alec told her about the coin deal. The frown deepened. She turned to the young man.

"If you had more than sawdust between your ears, you'd have known better. Serves you right, though. You thought you were on to something, didn't you? Typical of your family!"

To Alec's surprise, the young man just shuffled his feet and looked embarrassed. Kim turned to Alec.

"You get off home. I'll settle up here and you can pay me back out of your pocket money. And you lay off fiddling. We don't do that sort of thing, whatever other folks do."

Alec wasted no more time, but ran off down the road. As he reached the corner, he looked back. Kim and the young man were still talking.

10

Flash Bowden – Night Rider

"So you see, Abu, you're a theoretical possibility, but a practical impossibility," said Alec.

"But I believe in you," he added hastily.

"Big thrills," replied Abu.

"You know, Abu, you're getting very slangy lately. Are you reading my comics on the sly?"

Abu did not answer. Alec, who was lying on the bed, too idle to get up and get undressed for the night, picked up the can and peered inside.

"Do you know, Abu, I think you're offended, but I can't see you. It's a nuisance really. Why can't you materialize, just once, to please me?"

Abu sighed.

"It has always been my fate. Ever since I began to work as a genie, my masters always became unreasonable in the end."

"Oh, all right, forget it. But I must say I'm beginning to lose confidence in you and your instamatic miracles. I mean, apart from providing me with shish kebab now and then and the odd half-ton of sherbet, what have you done except get me into trouble and disgrace me in public?"

"Oh, ungrateful . . ." groaned Abu. "Did I not free you from the menace of one Ginger Wallace?"

"Ginger Wallace?" Alec leapt off the bed. "What do you mean?"

"Did I not strike him with the Great Itch so that he must stay home and not cloud your days at school?"

"Oh no, Abu! Was it you who did that? Well, you shouldn't have." Alec was torn between guilt and glee. Then a thought struck him.

"But what if the rest of the family catch it, you idiot genie?"

Abu was offended now. "That Great Itch is not a plague. It descends only upon those who are chosen."

"I wish I knew whether to trust you or not."

Abu was silent.

"Look, Abu, I'll give you a chance. We'll kill two birds with one stone. You lift the curse from Ginger Wallace and take me over to their house now, so I can check up that they're all OK. Only, they mustn't see me, get it?"

Abu grunted, "The Great Itch cannot be removed."

"Oh yes it can. You put it on, you take it off." Alec was so masterful that he surprised himself.

"Oh, as you will," replied Abu reluctantly, "but the curse must endure for seven days."

Alec did a quick count on his fingers. "That means Ginger will be OK by Sunday. Now," he added, "I'm ready for a quick, invisible trip to the Wallaces, Number 85, Boner's Street."

"Thy will . . .' said Abu, and the room vanished. Alec had a sensation of flying with the wind

92

whistling past him, but before he had a chance to enjoy it, he had landed.

"Hey, Abu, where are we?"

He was in a bedroom with an old broken sash window, which let in light from a street lamp outside. In its glow he could see that the room was very untidy; bits of furniture, old clothes, newspapers, cups, saucers and plates were all lying about.

"Who's that?"

Alec stared. Someone was sitting up in bed, a woman with her hair in curlers and her thin shoulders showing through a tattered nightie.

"Who's there?" she wheezed.

Alec goggled. Oh no, Abu strikes again. They had come to the wrong floor. They were in Miss Morris's bedroom and the old lady had woken up.

"I don't care who you are, I'll have you as soon as I've got my specs on."

The old lady jerked back her bedclothes and with astonishing agility launched herself out of bed towards Alec. "That's funny," she muttered, "I was sure someone was there. It'll be one of them poltergeists Harry Bowden was talking about." Shaking her head, Miss Morris clambered back into bed.

"Quick, Abu, you Great Arabian Plonker. Get us out of here and upstairs to the Wallaces," whispered Alec.

The room disappeared and re-formed. Now it was long and narrow and very dark. Because there was no light from the street, Alec guessed they were now at the back of the house. He could just make out a bed and a cot. In the bed he thought he could see Eulalia.

She lay on her back, one arm awkwardly behind her head, the other cradling a smaller dark head on the pillow beside her. It must be one of her sisters.

Alec moved over to the door which barely opened. He saw why. The bed would have to be shifted round first because there wasn't room. He shook his head. This beat the boxroom any day of the week. The baby in the cot whimpered. Eulalia stirred in her sleep, sat up slowly, drawing her arm carefully from under her sister's neck. Then she slid her feet out of bed and tiptoed over to the cot making shushing noises.

Alec called to Abu and a second later he was lying on his own bed again. It was some while before he got to sleep.

Next day in line-up, Eulalia and her friends giggled and whispered as they passed him. "Believe it or not, I had a dream about him last night."

"Who?"

"Little Skinny over there. He stood right by my bed, staring at me."

"Why, you're not safe even in your own bed, are you?"

Mrs Wyatt, the PE mistress, came charging down the line. "Quiet there!"

One of Eulalia's friends muttered under her breath. Mrs Wyatt heard though, and advanced on the girl.

"I heard that. Let me tell you, I've eaten people like you for breakfast before."

"Oh, Miss. It's *us* who are supposed to be cannibals, not you," said Eulalia impulsively.

94

Mrs Wyatt looked grim for a moment, then grinned.

"All right. You win that one. Now get inside."

That night Kim was late home from work and teatime passed quietly. But just as Alec was going up to his room, Dad, who had been reading the local paper as usual, exploded with laughter.

"Do you see this about Hetty Morris?"

Mum looked surprised.

" 'Another case of poltergeists reported by a senior citizen of Bugletown. Miss Hetty Morris, of Boner's Street, reports that on Thursday night, after she had gone to bed, she became aware of a mysterious presence in her room. A search of the room disclosed nothing, but Miss Morris declared, "I'm sure someone was there."

" 'This follows the case reported in last week's *Gazette*, involving Mr Henry Bowden of the Roundhill Estate.' "

Dad put the paper down and laughed. Alec had never seen him laugh so much before.

"I might have known it. If our Dad had a poltergeist, Hetty Morris would have one too."

He stopped as he saw Mum glare at him.

"What's up then, Connie?"

"It's no laughing matter."

"How d'you mean? You don't believe all this about Hetty Morris seeing a ghost, do you?"

"No," said Mum, impatiently. "I mean what's happening to Miss Morris isn't funny."

Dad looked puzzled.

"I don't know what you're getting at, love."

"No, that daft story in the *Gazette* reminded me. Hetty Morris came here this afternoon. She's very upset. She says the council man has been round to tell them that Boner's Street is coming down and they're all being shifted out to Moorside."

"Well?"

"Well, she doesn't want to go, that's what. And you can't blame her."

"No, but what's all the rush? They've been talking for donkey's years about pulling down Boner's Street."

"She says it's something to do with the Health Department as well as Councillor Blaggett."

"Hey, wait a minute! There's something in the *Gazette* here. Front page and all," said Dad, picking up the paper again.

" 'Mystery sickness, among immigrants in Bugletown' " – that's the headline. 'Reports of an undiagnosed illness among black tenants of Boner's Street took Council Health and Housing Department officials to the area this week. While the authorities stress that there is no cause for concern, the presence of the illness, which does not appear to be infectious, has raised again the question of the future of the tenants in this street which has been marked down for clearance . . .

" 'Councillor Blaggett told our reporter, "We are not overlooking the possibility of sickness being brought into the area, perhaps by an illegal immigrant." ' "

Dad threw down the paper again.

"That man talks a lot of rubbish. If it's not infectious, how can it have been brought into the area?"

"I don't know that I'm all that interested in that. I'm more interested in poor old Miss Morris. She was so upset this afternoon that she was in tears."

Dad shook his head. "I don't see why they have to move the whole street out to Moorside, just because someone's been ill."

"I'll tell you why, our Dad," said Kim as she breezed in through the kitchen doorway and pulled off her scarf.

"Ah, the late Kim Bowden," said Mum.

"Don't be sarky now, Mum," said Kim. "I've just been talking to Arthur Blaggett."

"Surprise us," said Mum, but Kim ignored the comment.

"He reckons there's a big scheme on. They want all that area around Boner's and Upshaw Street for high-rise flats, executive flats they call them, for people working at the refinery they're supposed to be building on the Penfold Road. And I'll tell you what. They're getting rid of the Tank at last, and turning it into a big car park."

"Car park?" said Mum. "Whatever for? They've got that big place at the corner of Station Road and School Lane."

"Ah, that's going to be turned into a big shopping centre, all linked up with the flats. This area's going up in the world," said Kim.

"But," Alec broke in excitedly, "they can't use the Tank for a car park. It's got no road in or out."

"It hasn't now," replied Mum. "But it did have at one time. They used to take stuff in and out under the railway arches door and along Boner's Street and School Lane to the main road. When they closed the Tank down, they boarded up the arches. Anyway, it's about time the Tank was cleared. Nothing but an eyesore."

"But they can't do that," said Alec.

"You get off upstairs and finish your homework, our Alec," said his mother. "It's got nothing to do with you."

Alec banged out into the passage. Nothing to do with him, indeed! They couldn't take the Tank and turn it into a mouldy old car park. The sound of voices from the kitchen stopped him again.

"What do they want a big shopping centre for?" demanded Mum. "All that expense for nothing."

"Oh, that's probably not for some time yet," said Kim. "But I reckon they'll clear Boner's Street pretty soon. Councillor Blaggett and his mates are dead set on those executive flats."

"So poor old Hetty Morris and the others have to move out. Well, it's not fair," said Mum, "and somebody ought to tell them so."

"What are you looking at me like that for?" asked Dad.

"Well, why don't you lot up at the Railway Club do something?"

"Huh, them," said Kim, "all they ever do is argue the toss whether diesel trains are better than electric."

Alec heard Dad get up and put his paper aside.

"I'm going out," said Dad.

Alec nipped up to his room, changed out of his school clothes into his jumper and jeans and charged out of the house, ignoring his mother's shout of, "What about your homework?"

He was heading towards the Tank when he heard someone call him. It was Granddad, busy hoeing a row of beans on the allotment. The old man leaned on the hoe and grinned at him.

"You look as though you've lost half a crown and found sixpence. Come here, lad, and tell us about it."

Alec hesitated.

"Please yourself," said Granddad, and started to attack the weeds again.

Alec drifted over to the allotment and Granddad stopped work again. Alec told him about the argument in the kitchen.

"Ah," he nodded. "That's bad about Hetty Morris, poor old soul. But you remember, last week, she wanted to ship those black people out to Moorside. Well, her wish has been granted, though not the way she wanted. That's how it goes. But what are you so upset about the Tank for? It's an eyesore. Always was."

Alec was silent. Even Granddad wouldn't understand about the Tank.

Granddad went on, "It'd be more to the point if they cleaned up that canal and had a recreation centre with boats and all on it. And opened up those arches so that people could see a bit what's on the other side of the railway."

Alec listened, then thought for a moment.

"Mum and Kim were on to our Dad about

99

Miss Morris, Why won't he do anything, Granddad? Whatever happens, he just sits there and says nothing. Then he puts his paper down and goes out to the Club."

Granddad laughed.

"You don't reckon much to your dad, eh?"

Alec reddened.

"I didn't say that."

"Well, I'll tell you something for nothing, lad. He didn't reckon much to his dad either."

Alec stared.

"His dad . . . How do you mean, Granddad?"

"When you say your dad never has anything to say for himself, his dad was just the opposite, when your dad was a boy. Always talking, always shouting the odds. There wasn't a subject under the sun he didn't reckon to know all about, whether he did or he didn't. I think your dad had it right up to here," Granddad gestured at his chin, "with his dad and his talk, talk, talk. Which is maybe why he keeps his mouth shut, now."

Alec stared at Granddad.

"My dad's dad. But that's . . ."

Granddad grinned.

"That's right. Your dad used to be right fed up with me at times."

He turned back to his weeding. Alec wandered off. Life, he could see, was going to get more complicated the older he got.

It was funny, he thought. When Dad was a lad . . . Granddad was his dad . . . and when . . .

He gave up.

11

Abu Puts in an Appearance

Alec was still brooding over everything when he went to school on Monday. He was so deep in thought that he hardly noticed that Ginger Wallace hadn't come back to school. He mooned his way through lessons that day, fortunately without disasters, and his mind was still churning away when he set out for home.

Lost to the world, he wandered along Boner's Street. What was he doing there? He'd forgotten his emergency rule to go home by Station Road. Still, he'd gone too far to go back now. He pressed on, keeping a wary eye open, until he reached the railway arches with their dark plank barrier.

He stood still in the road and looked at them. Suddenly the words of Granddad came back into his mind. "Open up those arches so that people can see a bit what's on the other side."

Suddenly he knew what he would do. He would ask Abu Salem for one last piece of instamagic. After that he would allow Abu to go back into the can and sleep a million years if he wanted. It would be a bargain and it would be worth it.

He dropped his satchel, pulled out the can, and

with a mixed feeling of excitement and regret, he rubbed the top of it and whispered,

"Salaam Aleikum, O Abu Salem.."

"Aleikum Salaam, O Alec. Keef Haalak?"

"IlHamdulilaah."

"What is thy will?" Abu sounded wary.

"I want one last piece of super, king-size, family pack, transformation magic from you, Abu, and after that I shall resign as your master and you can go to sleep."

"By the Beard of the Prophet," said Abu, "that must be a mighty spell. Never have I known a master release his slave before. If it be in my power, it shall be. Speak on, O Alec."

Alec spoke on, and Abu heard him in silence. At last . . .

"That is a great wish, O Alec. Since you wish it for others and not for yourself, I shall perform what I can."

Alec stood in Boner's Street, holding the can. A minute passed. Then the ground began to heave like an earthquake. In front of him the railway arches began to quiver and shake, like a dream sequence on the telly. One by one the arches opened, showing the blue sky beyond, and on the slopes he saw the estate and his home appear. The Tank, with its mouldering brickwork, its rusty iron, its dank shrubs and weeds, its oozy canal, had vanished like smoke in the air.

In its place was a long low hall with bright windows, a football pitch, tennis courts and archery butts. Beyond it all, a waterway gleamed in the sun and boats bobbed on the water where the crane house had been. The great plank fence had fallen away and instead there were trees and flower beds. From the corner of his eye, Alec saw Boner's Street and gasped. The tall houses were newly painted, the high stone steps shone white, the windows caught the sun. The piles of rubbish and the broken-down cars had vanished. At the end of the street had appeared a clear space with swings, slides and a high commando climbing net. It was fantastic. Who would have believed Boner's Street and the Tank could look like this?

He ran forward. One thing he could claim for himself; he would be first to go on one of those boats on the canal. But even as he ran, a fog dropped over the Tank covering everything. In the midst of the fog, someone called him.

"Help, help, O Alec, help!"

Alec turned so swiftly he nearly fell. The fog was clearing, or rather it shrank together into a small space just a yard or two away from him. As it cleared, the outline of Boner's Street and the railway arches appeared. Alec saw, much to his dismay, that they were just as they had always been, dark, grim, mucky, rubbish strewn. Nothing had changed.

Nothing?

From the shrinking patch of fog, a dark shape emerged, no bigger than a man. But a tall, broad-shouldered man. Alec could see him now.

He was dressed in a long red and white striped robe and flowing burnous, like one of the forty thieves in Ali Baba. On his feet he wore sandals and round his waist was a broad shining belt, into which was thrust a wicked curved sword.

But his face was dark brown. A silly thought went through Alec's head. I thought he was an Arab or something, but of course he was a slave from Africa.

Then Alec burst out,

"Abu, what happened?"

"Aieee, O Alec. The worst has happened. In my great effort to work your will, the magic spell proved too much. In trying to make it work, something, alas, has gone astray, and here I am, materialized."

Alec looked round in alarm. The idea of a black slave in ancient robes standing in the middle of Boner's Street was at first quite funny. On the other hand it could be very awkward.

"I think you'd best disappear again and finish off the spell."

"Alas, if I disappear again, it will take all my power and I will not be able to work the spell. For the moment my powers are so low that I can do neither. I must stay with you, I fear. But that was your first wish, that you should see me," the genie added cheerfully.

"Oh, Nora," said Alec. "What am I going to do? You are a flipping nuisance, Abu."

A hurt look passed over the black man's face and Alec was immediately ashamed.

"I'm sorry, Abu. I didn't mean to be rotten. It's just that now I don't know what to do. I mean, I can't tell you to get back in the can and carry you home, can I? And you can't stay here in Boner's Street. Someone'll come along any minute."

Abu shrugged. "Truly, O Alec, I am sorry, but I cannot help it. In the Great Book of Magic, every genie is warned that there is a limit to his powers. I have been lucky. I have known genies who tried to do too much and they exploded and were never seen or heard of again."

"Oh, I'm glad that didn't happen to you. Now what can we do? I could smuggle you home and ask Granddad to put you up in the caravan. No, that would only cause more trouble."

Suddenly Alec had an idea.

"I'll take you to my hideout, Abu. Come on."

Picking up his satchel, he led the way across the road to the arches. Beneath the sign BUGLETOWN ORDNANCE – KEEP OUT Alec found the fourteenth board and gave it a push, but it would not move. Alec remembered that the day Ginger and his mates had tried to follow him, he had blocked up the entrance. He beckoned to Abu and swiftly explained the problem. Abu pushed back the sleeves of his robes which revealed his huge, muscular, brown arms. With one thrust he pushed in the loose plank, shoving aside the brickwork which jammed it.

Alec prepared to slip through. But, what about Abu? He'd never get through. It was too narrow. They'd have to move another board. Abu must have been a thought reader. He dug his fingers under the end of the plank and gave a terrific push and pull. With a shriek, the nails gave and the second plank swung inwards, leaving a space wide enough for both of them to go through.

"Hey. What are you doing down there? Hooligans!"

It was Miss Morris. Her voice screeched down the road and Alec could hear her boots clumping along the pavement.

"Quick, Abu, in we go."

They wasted no time. In two seconds they were through into the Tank and Abu pushed the two planks back into place, covering the entrance.

"Now where did they go? I could have sworn I saw them smashing the fence in. A big black fella and somebody else." They could hear Miss Morris muttering to herself on the other side of the fence. Alec beckoned to Abu and they walked over to the main factory buildings where they climbed the rickety stairs and entered the crane room. Abu looked about him.

"What place is this? An ancient palace?"

Alec looked blank. How could he explain factory to Abu? "Oh, it's just an old place where people used to work. No one ever comes here now.

"It's not very comfortable, but it's safe. Did you say the old magic power was completely gone, or will it come back?" he asked Abu.

"I know not. Perhaps."

Abu looked grim, so Alec changed the subject.

"Well, I'll have to see what I can do to find you some food and blankets, though where and how I don't know."

"Fear not, O Alec. What you can do, you will do, I know."

"Anyway, Abu, you hang on, while I sneak off home and find what I can. Ma'asalaama."

"Ma'asalaama," replied Abu, as Alec went down the stairs.

As Alec crossed the canal, he thought that it was some little time since he had kept his disasters—triumphs score card. Mind you, disasters had put so many in the net that it was hardly worth bothering. Instead he concentrated on solving Abu's problems.

He worked out a simple plan. He would nip into the caravan and borrow two blankets from one of the lockers. Granddad had plenty and the others were only used in the middle of winter when the family needed extra. When he'd done that, he'd have a scout round the larder and see what he could rustle up.

The plan was fine, if it had worked. Granddad was out, and picking up the blankets was not difficult. Alec was in the middle of raiding the larder when Mum caught him. Two minutes of third degree and she'd found out about the blankets.

He couldn't tell her what they were for, but pretended he had a scheme for camping out for the night. It was daft and Mum clearly didn't believe it. She said nothing more, but sent him upstairs to get on with his homework and told him he needn't think about going out again that evening.

Up in his room, Alec counted his money. He had enough (ignoring the fact that he owed Kim seventy-five pence) to buy half a take-away kebab at Nick's café in Station Road. He wondered if they sold half a kebab; perhaps he could put a deposit on one and pay by instalments.

"This is getting us nowhere, Bowden," he told himself and had to admit that he was right. But what to do? He couldn't leave old Abu in the lurch, even if he wasn't the most successful genie in the fourth dimension. Now he knew the meaning of the words "spell disaster".

Alec sat on his bed and pondered for half an hour. But at the end of it he was still left with the same daft situation. Aladdin never had to look after his slave like that. Funny, the more he thought of Abu as a slave, the more ridiculous it seemed. Abu was a friend, a mate. They'd had some fun together. Now the boot was on the other foot and Alec Bowden had to work the magic.

"That's life," he said, addressing the empty can he held in his hand. It was truly empty now.

"One moment you have a genie at your command. Next moment you have an illegal immigrant on your hands." Yes, Councillor Blaggett was right after all. There was an illegal immigrant around Boner's Street, and Alec Bowden had brought him there.

"Illegal immigrant" meant Abu had to be kept a secret. But Alec couldn't just leave him down in the Tank. Abu would be cold and hungry in the crane room. Alec would have to get help. But who could he ask?

Not the family. It wouldn't be fair to get Grand-dad mixed up in all this, though Alec was sure the old man would help. Not Kim, either. She was too friendly with Councillor Blaggett's son these days.

He was on his feet, tramping round the room, when the thought struck him. There was only one person in Bugletown, or rather two, whom he could ask to help Abu. The thought hit him right in the middle of the stomach like a wet fish.

But it had to be, it had to . . .

It had to be Eulalia and Ginger Wallace.

12

"Poor Little Ginger"

Coronation Street was booming away on the telly as Alec slipped downstairs and into the kitchen. All was quiet. He gently eased open the larder door.

"Is that you, Alec?" called his mother from the front room. What a radar system!

"Just getting myself a peanut butter sandwich, Mum."

"All right, love. Straight upstairs again afterwards."

Alec didn't answer. He wasn't going upstairs but couldn't bring himself to fib about it. He made two sandwiches, one with fish paste and one with peanut butter, and nicked a plastic bag to wrap them in. He squashed the bag into his jeans pocket.

The back door was open. The evening was still light and not too cold. If he got down to the Tank right away . . .

"Psst. Where are you off to, Alec?"

Granddad was peering out through the caravan window.

"Nowhere special, Granddad," whispered Alec.

The caravan door opened. Granddad's arm appeared holding a blanket.

"Please yourself. Take this with you, though. And hey, tell us about it afterwards."

"Oh, thanks a lot, Granddad. That's smashing. But how did you know?"

"I heard your mother talking to you in the kitchen. Now, you'd best get off before the programme ends."

Waving to Grandad, Alec ran off along the road, past the allotments and down to the plank fence round the Tank. It looked solid enough now, and it seemed impossible that for one tiny moment, all this had disappeared and a supersonic, marine fun centre had been in its place. Now all that was left was the Tank and poor old Abu shivering in his satin nightie.

The thought made him speed up. Up went the loose plank and Alec went through the fence like a Commando. He was over the canal in a flash and the bridge was firm this time. Another few seconds and he ran up the rickety stairs of the crane house.

"Abu," he called. There was no answer.

"Abu," he called again, bursting into the crane room.

To his relief a loud snore answered him. Abu, knees tucked under his chin, was fast asleep on the table. Alec shook him.

"Aieee," grunted the genie, stretching himself and nearly falling off the table. He looked round wildly for a moment and shook his head in bewilderment. Then he grinned. Alec put the blanket on the table, pulled out the squashed sandwiches from his jeans pocket, and he offered them to Abu.

"Shukran jazilan, O Alec."

Abu disposed of the sandwiches in four massive bits. He slapped his stomach and, holding out his hand, shook Alec's hand.

"Look, Abu. I'm afraid you'll have to stay here and keep out of sight for a while."

"Why, O Alec? Am I not fit to be seen?"

"No, well, er, people like you aren't . . ."

Oh, how do you explain about illegal immigrants to someone who's never heard of race relations?

"Look, Abu, I'm going to see someone, to ask for help."

"Ah, someone with wealth and power?"

"Not exactly. But someone who might know what to do."

"I am in your hands, O Alec."

"OK. I'm off. Keep out of sight. Ma'asalaama!"

"Ma'asalaama!" Abu replied.

Alec rushed down the stairs and out across the waste to the fence on the Boner's Street side.

It took him a few minutes to pull out the planks which Abu had forced into place that afternoon and push his way out into Boner's Street. He went carefully, for he didn't want Miss Morris to catch sight of him. A pound to a penny, the old lady would report what she'd seen earlier that day to someone or other.

There was no one in sight as he hurried down the street to Number 85, but as he came closer, he saw someone whom he guessed must be Mrs Wallace.

She sat comfortably on top of the old stone steps, knitting away with two little girls in pinnies and pigtails sitting beside her. Mrs Wallace was calling across the street to a friend who sat mending clothes on the steps of the house opposite. As he came nearer, Alec heard something that stopped him in his tracks.

"Yes, poor little Ginger," called Mrs Wallace.

The other woman nodded.

"Poor Ginger."

"Yes, he had to be taken today. We couldn't do anything for him."

Alec tiptoed past the Wallaces' steps in a state of shock. Poor Ginger . . . had to be taken . . . couldn't do anything. Oh no! What had happened?

Abu had promised him that Ginger wouldn't come to any harm. But if he had, Abu wouldn't be able to put matters right. If anything serious had happened to Ginger, thought Alec, it's all my fault.

"Right, Bowden. Say your prayers."

Alec nearly jumped out of his jeans. Coming out of the passage at the side of Number 85 was Ginger Wallace, large as life, or being Ginger, rather larger.

Alec thought of running. He had ten yards' start, but Ginger was an athlete. Anyway, he'd come to see Ginger and that's what he'd do. He turned to face his enemy who ploughed on at him like a tank.

"Look, Ginger . . ."

But Ginger swung, a long right, just like Mohammad Ali. Luckily for Alec, the aim wasn't world championship class. Ginger's fist struck him square on the pocket which held the trusty can. Alec doubled up, winded. But Ginger whistled with pain and brought his injured fist up to his mouth.

"Serve you right, Byron Wallace," said a laughing voice behind them.

Coming across the road was Eulalia. Alec was always glad to see her, but never more than now.

"Byron?" he gasped.

"Oh, yes," said Eulalia. "He's baptized Byron Churchill Wallace. And," she spoke more quietly, "don't let our mother hear you call him Ginger, or she'll skin you! I mean it."

Alec looked nervously round. But Mrs Wallace was placidly rocking one of the little girls on her lap and did not seem to have heard. The neighbours had gone indoors.

"But what was your mum saying, as I was coming up the road, about poor old Ginger?"

Eulalia's laugh echoed down the road.

"We have a ginger cat. At least we did have till today. Our Byron stayed off school today to take it to the vet, poor little thing."

Alec looked at Ginger who was standing neutrally by.

"But I thought you had been ill."

Ginger shrugged. "I was sick the whole week. The doctor said it was some sort of flu, nothing to it really. Why are you so interested in my health, Skinny?"

"Because it said in the papers there was a mysterious illness in Boner's Street."

Ginger looked contemptuous. "I think that old girl downstairs has been talking too much. She doesn't like us."

Alec nodded.

"Anyway," Ginger became aggressive again, "what are you doing down Boner's Street?"

"I came to see you and Eulalia," said Alec, his nervousness returning.

"Oh, now isn't that flattering." said Eulalia. Then she chuckled, "But be careful. He doesn't like just anyone talking to his sister."

"Belt up," said Ginger. Eulalia looked her brother squarely in the eye.

"You might scare Skinny, but you don't scare me."

"Huh," replied Ginger, but left it at that. He turned to Alec.

"Anyway, what do you want us for?"

"I want your help." Ginger's eyebrows rose. "I mean, I need your help, badly. It's for a friend – a – er, black friend."

"Black friend?" Ginger was immediately suspicious.

"Look," said Alec. "Can you keep a secret?"

"That depends."

"Listen. Remember that day you chased me by the railway arches and couldn't catch me?"

Ginger nodded.

"There's a way through. It leads to an old works called the Tank, where I have my secret place."

Ginger began to look interested. Eulalia listened quietly.

"The point is, my friend – he's called Abu Salem – is there. He shouldn't really be here in Bugletown at all."

"Where's he from?" Ginger was still suspicious, but interested.

"I can't really say." He couldn't say out of a beer can from tenth-century Baghdad. "But will you come?"

"How do we know you haven't a mob up there waiting for us?"

Alec appealed to Eulalia. "Honest. There's no trick. I didn't start that trouble at school. That was Spotty Sam and he's not even a friend of mine. I've never told anyone else about this secret place except my friend and he's living away at Moorside now."

Eulalia nodded. "That's where the council wants to send us all now."

Ginger shrugged. "OK, but we'll be using that Tank place from now on."

Alec felt a pang inside. Still it couldn't be helped. He had to do this, for Abu's sake.

"Come on then."

"Where are you two going?" Mrs Wallace called.

"Just down the road to look at a place, Ma," replied Eulalia.

"Don't be long."

"Ten minutes."

The three of them walked silently down the road to the railway arches. Alec stopped by the old Bugletown Ordnance notice and looked round.

"Must keep a look out for Miss Morris. She saw

116

Abu and me go in here this afternoon. She thinks we're up to something."

He pushed back the two planks. Ginger squatted down and looked through the gap. He whistled.

"Some secret you got here, Skinny." Ginger pushed his way through, Eulalia followed and Alec came last. As they picked their way through the tangle of woods and old junk, Alec explained that the Tank had been a factory which had been closed down. Now he'd heard they planned to turn it into a car park.

"That'll be a lot of use, up in Moorside," said Eulalia.

When they came to the main building, Ginger stopped.

"Now, before we go in there, I reckon you'd better tell us the whole story about this friend of yours."

Alec nodded.

"OK, I'll do that. You won't believe it, but I'll tell you."

He told them the story as briefly as he could. He could see they thought he was kidding, but they listened anyway. Why not? It was worth hearing, even if it was impossible.

But Ginger wasn't impressed.

"You reckon this genie-man's upstairs in the old crane room? They have better stories on the telly."

Alec suddenly became angry.

"Please yourself. Are you coming up to see, or are you scared?"

Ginger frowned, but Eulalia smiled.

"Skinny's got you there, Byron. Touched you on your tenderest spot."

"OK," said Ginger, "lead the way."

As they came through the crane room door, Abu was curled up as usual, snoring away. At the sight of his red and white robes, Ginger burst into delighted laughter.

"Hey, what's this dude doing in fancy dress?"

Abu uncurled, shot upright and reaching out a huge fist, grabbed Ginger by his shirt.

"By the Beard of the Prophet!" he swore.

Ginger grinned.

"Man, a Black Muslim."

13

We're Being Followed

Abu gently released Ginger and smiled.

"Aha, Alec, you have other slaves, then?"

"Cool it," said Ginger, the smile going from his face.

"No, no, Abu. They're friends, like me."

"He means we're British, even if we are black," said Eulalia. She smiled as if it were a joke, but Alec could see she didn't think it was funny. Abu turned to Alec again.

"So there are black British and white British? Then why must Abu Salem hide away?"

Alec groaned. How could he explain? But Ginger cut in.

"Our people come here from Jamaica, in the Caribbean. When this country owned the lot out there, and our people stayed at home, they didn't mind us being British. But when our people started coming over here, they changed their tune."

"It's not as simple as that, Ginger," said Alec. Ginger turned on him.

"Maybe not to you, but it is to me."

Eulalia flapped her hands.

"You don't help old Abu at all by rowing. The

thing is, Abu, you don't have a passport, documents, nothing. And without permit papers, you're not allowed in the country, even if you think you should be. You're just plain and simple illegal."

Abu nodded. That he understood.

Ginger slowly simmered down and became coolly practical. "We could smuggle him into Boner's Street and say he's a cousin over on a visit. Round here, people can't tell the difference," he added, shooting a glance at Alec.

Eulalia shook her head. "It sounds simple, but just now we've got the council man nosing around. No, we've got to ask someone."

Ginger looked worried. "Like Pa, you mean. He's not going to like that, not at all."

"Maybe I can have a word with Ma," said Eulalia, thoughtfully. "See, Abu, if you can bear sleeping in this dump tonight, we'll sneak up here tomorrow morning with more food. And then, tomorrow night, we'll see if we can find somewhere else decent for you. OK?"

Abu bowed his thanks.

"Look, Skinny," Eulalia went on, "is there another way out of this place?"

Alec nodded. "There's a gap in the fence over the canal."

"Right. Well, you go one way and Byron and I'll go the other. If people see you with us in Boner's Street, someone's going to get suspicious. We'll let you know in school tomorrow what we can do. Right?"

"Yes," said Alec. "You going first?"

Eulalia smiled as she and Ginger moved towards the door.

"Don't worry, Skinny. We won't tell anyone else about your place, will we?" She nudged her brother, who winked at Alec. Then they were off down the stairs, leaving Alec with Abu.

"Truly, this is a strange land, O Alec."

"You can say that again, O Abu."

"Truly, this is a . . ."

"Oh, never mind, Abu. Will you be warm enough with that one blanket? With luck it'll only be for tonight."

"I shall sleep as a babe." And Abu hoisted himself on to the table again, and prepared to curl up, almost as though he were inside the beer can.

Alec felt the can in his pocket as he said good night and went off down the stairs. It wasn't much use now, but he was going to hang on to it for sentimental reasons.

As soon as he woke up the next day, Alec had his familiar feeling of disaster. This was not just because last night Mum had caught him sneaking in and had stopped this week's pocket money, but his early warning system told him that bigger disasters were on the way, bigger than any he had known. Catastrophe was just round the corner. He'd lost the paddle and he was drifting towards Niagara Falls.

Still, he had to go through with it. At least he'd spent last night in his warm bed, not curled up on the crane room table. What a come-down for a genie!

He arrived at school just in time to catch the line-up.

Eulalia passed him a note in the corridor.

"Aha," said Ronnie Carter, "the Casanova of 3F strikes again."

"Drop dead," said Alec savagely.

"Pardon me for breathing," came the reply. Alec ignored Ronnie and hurried away.

In Assembly Mr Foster was reading the lesson. With his head in the clouds as usual, Mr Foster had chosen some passage from the Book of Kings, which might have been a rave 5,000 years ago, but was not keyed into the twentieth century. Boredom set in. Alec fiddled Eulalia's note out of his pocket and read it.

"We move Abu this evening. Meet us after school by the station."

He slid the note back into his pocket just as Mr Cartwright made a reconnaissance run down the ranks. Mr Foster rambled his way through the rest of the Old Testament and they were dismissed. The day began to grind on.

Grind on was the word: maths – double science – English. Alec tried to keep his mind on his work and stay out of trouble. He must avoid being kept in. Someone leant over his desk.

"What's on your mind, Alec?" Miss Welch asked.

"Er, nothing, Miss," said Alec.

"Then why have you written the last sentence three times?"

"Just trying to get it right, Miss."

"But it's wrong all three times, Alec."

122

Oh no.

As Miss Welch wandered away again, Alec heard Ronnie Carter murmur, "What does Bowden have that other men don't? It can't be his tobacco. It can't be his after-shave. But all the best looking women just hover around him."

Alec's ruler caught him neatly behind the ear. Ronnie yelped.

"Ronald Carter, are you ill?" asked Miss Welch.

"Just a bit of cramp, Miss," replied Ronnie. Reaching down behind him, he took Alec's foot and twisted it.

"Gerroff!" cursed Alec and kicked at the torturing hand. Miss Welch homed in like a rocket.

"What *is* going on here?"

"Sorry, Miss. It's my foot. It got caught."

Miss Welch glared at them both.

"Lucky for you two, I'm a gentle soul. Stop grinning, or I'll bang your heads together. Imagine that," she addressed the class. "What sort of a noise would it make? Maybe we could use it in the Christmas Play instead of coconuts."

Alec breathed again. The danger was past. He looked at the clock. Why did time go slower on one day than another? He must ask Mr Jameson about that.

But the afternoon did pass finally. The class was dismissed and Alec cleared the school gates like a space rocket leaving the pad at Cape Kennedy. On his way to the station he called in at the baker's in Station Road and bought two meat pies.

He hoped they were mutton or horse or something,

but not pork. Muslims didn't eat pork, or was that Jewish people? He couldn't remember. There were so many different ways of offending people, once you started. Still, he couldn't discuss the matter with the baker. He left the shop and raced along the street to the station, where Eulalia and Ginger were waiting.

"Where've you been, Skinny?"

Alec waved the meat pies.

"Listen," said Ginger. "We have to go into the Tank from your side this time."

"Why?"

"Because last night we were spotted coming out the Boner's Street side by Miss Morris. And she had a creep from the council, one of Blaggett's spies, with her."

"Oh, no!" said Alec. "What did they say?"

"Didn't say anything," answered Eulalia.

"They just pointed, so we split. We didn't wait to ask them to explain."

Alec's early warning system was right; there was trouble brewing.

"Come on," said Eulalia. "Let's go. We've got a plan. But it can keep until we see Abu."

"Hey," said Alec. "Did you take him some food this morning?"

"Of course we did. What do you think we are? We said we would, and we did."

"Sorry," murmured Alec. They hurried on under Station Bridge out on to the Penfold Road, and the turned left into the estate. As they walked up the hill, Alec could see that some people were staring at them. It couldn't be helped. But they'd have to be careful getting through the fence into the Tank.

"This way," said Alec, when they reached the top of the hill and turned down the path past the allotments. There was no one about round here. They stopped by the high fence and Alec began to count the planks.

"You've got this organized, Skinny," said Ginger.

Alec found the plank and pushed.

As he did, someone shouted from the top of the slope.

"Hey, you kids down there! What are you doing?"

Alec turned.

"Look," he said, "over the other side of the allotments."

"What is it?"

"It's Mr Hardcastle from the Housing Department and PC Hadley, that's all. And they're coming after us."

"Quick," said Ginger, "let's get through the fence."

"No," said Eulalia, "that'll lead them to Abu."

"It's OK," said Alec. "Pound to a penny, they can't get through this gap."

"Well, move then," said Ginger. "You first, Skinny."

Alec dived through, Eulalia came next, then Ginger. They had a struggle, for they were bigger than Alec was. But that only meant that Hadley and the council man couldn't get through at all.

"Quick," said Alec, "over the canal by my bridge."

"You two go over first," ordered Ginger, "then

I'll get rid of that plank. That'll make sure they can't follow."

"But how will you get over?" asked Alec, as they hurried down to the towpath.

"Oh, don't you worry about Wonder Boy," said Eulalia, as she scrambled over the bridge with Alec close behind her.

They turned on the other side of the canal to see Ginger take the plank in both hands, heave it up and let it sink in the green-black ooze. Then he turned and walked back towards the fence.

"Where's he going?" asked Alec. His question was answered as Ginger turned again and came running down, heading straight for the canal.

Alec's eyes opened wide as Ginger took off at the edge of the towpath and long-jumped the canal, landing in a heap about a yard away from them. He picked himself up, rubbed his hand and knocked the dust off his trousers.

"A good five metres, that."

"All right, Mr Olympic, 2000," said Eulalia. "We've got things to do."

The crane room was quiet as they climbed the stairs and opened the door. As Alec suspected, Abu was asleep and snoring gently, curled up on the table. *Sleeping* was Abu's second profession, Alec thought.

"Salaam Aleikum," he called.

"Aleikum Salaam," Abu replied, sitting upright.

"Keef Haalak?"

"IlHamdulilaah."

Eulalia grinned at Ginger.

"The boy's a genius."

Abu sat on the table, slowly stretching himself and scratching his stomach.

"You must be hungry, Abu," said Alec. "We've brought more food."

"Hungry? I could eat a horse," replied Abu.

"Who knows?" said Ginger. "You may do just that."

They set the packages on the table and opened them.

Abu's eyes gleamed. If he had any religious problems about meat, he must have been having a day off, because both the pies vanished along with the rest of the food, and the black coffee Eulalia had brought in a Thermos flask.

"A mighty feast," said Abu. "Why, you are all genies of the First Order."

"Listen, Abu," interrupted Alec. "We were followed when we came here, so we haven't much time. Now, Eulalia and Ginger have a plan which they'll tell you about."

Abu folded his arms.

"Speak on. I hear."

But Abu never heard what the plan might be, for right at that moment, from below, through the broken window of the crane room, they heard an angry bellow.

"They're up there in that old dump across the canal."

Alec leant forward and peered out of the corner of the window, for he recognized the voice.

Disaster had turned into catastrophe.

On the other side of the canal, waving his arms and pointing up at the crane room, was Councillor Blaggett.

14

The Siege of the Crane House

Yes, catastrophe had arrived in the person of Councillor Blaggett who was prowling up and down the far bank of the canal like a tiger. How had he managed to get through the gap in the fence? Councillor Blaggett was big and fat and looked rather like a rugby ball in clothes. He wore a long black coat and Homburg hat, for he was the chief undertaker in Bugletown and must have come straight from a funeral.

"How did he get in?" asked Alec.

Ginger crouched down beside him at the corner of the window. "They must have got the padlock off the gate," he said. Sure enough, the big gate stood open and in the gap were Mr Hardcastle and the broad figure of PC Hadley in his uniform.

"It's a full-scale boarding party," said Alec.

"Ah, but they can't get over," said Ginger.

"But for how long?" asked Eulalia from the other side of the crane room. Abu had changed into an old shirt and pair of jeans, and Eulalia was wrapping his robes up in a paper bag.

"Look, Ginge, can't you two sneak out at the Boner's Street side with Abu?"

"Not a chance. They'll see us when we get clear of the main building. We're stuck."

"Yes, but they don't know Abu's here now, do they? They only saw us three come in."

"Oh, they must know there's someone else here. They wouldn't make all this fuss over three kids," said Eulalia.

"So, what do we do?"

"We'll have to think of something. For the moment, they can't get over."

Councillor Blaggett must have been thinking along the same lines. He turned and shouted to the council man, "Go and get a plank or something so that we can get across."

"I can't see a plank anywhere, Mr Blaggett," came the reply. "There are a lot of planks on the other side," Mr Hardcastle added helpfully.

"Perhaps you'd like to go over and get one, then," said Councillor Blaggett sarcastically. PC Hadley turned away as though he were laughing.

"I can't see why you think it's so amusing, Constable." said Blaggett. "You haven't exactly been helpful so far."

The policeman placed his hands behind his back and looked over towards the crane house.

"I've been instructed to investigate reports that there is an illegal immigrant in this area. So far, I've seen three children, and I know who they are."

"I bet you do," muttered Ginger, peering out of the corner of the crane room window.

Councillor Blaggett strode up and down the canal

129

bank while Mr Hardcastle and the constable waited. Blaggett turned and said,

"Go up to one of the houses and see if you can borrow a plank. Hurry, man, hurry."

Mr Hardcastle hurried away through the open gate, while Blaggett went on with his pacing. He stopped by the massive iron structure of the crane gantry.

"Where does this ladder lead to?" he asked the constable. PC Hadley walked slowly and deliberately along the bank to stand by the councillor. He eyed the gantry up and down and from side to side and weighed the matter carefully.

"I think it was once used when they did maintenance work on the crane, sir."

"Then we can get across that way, can't we?"

"I'm not so sure about that, Mr Blaggett. Something of a skilled job, walking across a girder."

"Oh, nonsense, Hadley." Blaggett began to struggle out of his greatcoat, revealing a black suit underneath. He took off his jacket, folded both coats neatly, and placed them on the towpath. Then he began to roll up the sleeves of his snow-white shirt.

"Why doesn't he take his hat off?" said Ginger.

"I think he's a bit thin on top," whispered Alec.

Councillor Blaggett gripped one of the iron rungs of the ladder and, puffing gently, began to climb. PC Hadley put out a hand as though to stop him, and then thought better of it. He shrugged his shoulders and moved off a pace or two. Blaggett climbed and climbed, his face growing more red. But he did not stop.

"Man, he's got nerve," whispered Ginger.

"Look what he's doing now," said Alec.

Blaggett had reached the top of the ladder and paused for breath. The colour slowly returned to normal in his cheeks. Indeed he looked a little pale as he peered down into the greeny-black depths of the canal. But he hesitated only a second or two before he began to scramble on to the girder. Then, squatting down astride the iron, he began to inch his way over.

He had reached the middle of the girder, when the constable, who had been watching the gate, suddenly jerked up. The look of surprise on his face, upon seeing the councillor in mid-girder, made them all laugh.

"Sir, are you sure you should be doing that? It can't be very safe."

"Rubbish, Constable. There is something unauthorized going on in that building across the canal and I intend to get to the bottom of it," gasped Blaggett.

The councillor could hardly have put it better. For, right at that moment, he lost his balance on the girder. He grabbed wildly at the chains which hung from the small hand-operated crane, some three feet away. The effort only unbalanced him more. His hands missed the chains, while his legs lost their grip on the gantry.

With a "Look out!" from the constable and a groan from Blaggett, the large black-clad man dropped like a stone into the awful slimy depths of the canal. At that moment, Mr Hardcastle, with two men in overalls carrying scaffolding planks, hurried through the gate.

"Here we are, Mr Blaggett. This should cope with the canal," he called cheerfully.

But Councillor Blaggett, who was coping with the canal in his own way, gave no reply. He rose into sight from the black sludge. His beautiful hat was gone for ever, but round the centre of his pink, balding head, with its white cluster of curls, sat a dank skullcap of greasy mud.

On the bank the constable was struggling to take off his jacket. Mr Hardcastle, after a dumbstruck moment, began to run down to the side of the canal, the two other men following as quickly as they were able with the planks. The councillor with both arms raised to the sky, like a mad pop star, was slowly sliding down again into the gungey depths.

"Oh, can't we help him?" gasped Eulalia.

Alec had an inspiration.

"Quick, give me a hand, Ginge."

With Ginger's help, Alec freed the lever on the crane drum. It jerked forward, jammed, then jerked forward again.

Alec shouted to Eulalia over his shoulder, "You and Abu sneak off at the back. They'll never notice you with all this toing and froing."

"OK," shouted Eulalia. "Come on, Abu."

To Alec's relief, the chain unwound on the drum, slid along the crane arm and, with a rattling roar, dropped down towards the struggling Blaggett. Alec poked his head through one of the broken sections of the window.

"Sir," he called, "Mr Blaggett. Catch hold of the chain and we'll pull you up."

Councillor Blaggett looked up wildly, caught the chain with one hand, then the other, and held on like grim death. Then, to Alec and Ginger's amazement, he shouted, "There they are, Constable. In the crane house. Get the planks down, get across and catch them."

"Hey," said Ginger, "what a fanatic! He'd put his own mother in jail if she crossed the road on a green light."

"Give us a hand with the winding handle," said Alec. Together they grabbed the handle and began to heave. It was not easy. With Blaggett on the end, they were heaving a dead weight. But they managed to force the handle up and over, and once the drum began to revolve, the effort became easier. After a couple of minutes though they had to rest. Alec pressed down the brake handle with his foot and they looked out of the window. Councillor Blaggett was clear of the canal now. He hung in mid-air, a great bundle of sodden clothes, streaming with canal slime, his face streaked with ooze, his shirt a mouldy green colour. Even Mrs Blaggett wouldn't recognize him.

Along the canal bank, the council man and his assistants were busy fixing planks to repair the gap in Alec's bridge. The constable thought it his duty to remain on the towpath, anxiously watching the councillor, as he swung gently to and fro on the end of the chain.

"Are you lads sure you can handle that crane?" shouted PC Hadley.

"If we can't, it's all up with the councillor," shouted Ginger.

A red flush appeared beneath the treacly covering on the councillor's face.

"You impudent young . . ."

Ginger roared with laughter.

"Councillor, I love you. You're so black, you're almost beautiful!"

"Hey up. Don't upset him too much," warned Alec.

"Upset him? I'd like to," retorted Ginger. "What kind of a man is that? We save his life, and all he can think of is how he can get at us."

"Ah, well, Abu's away with Eulalia," replied Alec. "Have you got your puff back, Ginge? We'll start again if you have."

Ginger nodded. "Look, they've got the planks across now. They'll be over here in a minute."

They both leaned their weight on the winding handle and with a creak from the chains, Councillor Blaggett began his dignified ascent once more.

Suddenly from the distance, Alec heard,

"Daa-da-da-daa."

"Hey, what's that crazy hooting? I've heard it before from home, just when we're starting tea."

"It's my dad, bringing the 3.30 into Bugletown Station," answered Alec, feeling proud for some reason.

"He drives the diesel, eh? That's something. My dad's thought of getting a job on the railway."

"Why not?" said Alec. "Hey, look, Councillor Blaggett's nearly reached the top."

"Yes, look's like he's made it," grinned Ginger.

The councillor, his face no longer reddish-purple but grey-white beneath its crust of black muck, was reaching out now for the main crane girder.

"Think he'll be able to manage it on his own?" said Alec anxiously.

Ginger looked keenly along the girder. "He'll never do it. Look, Skinny. Can you hold this? I'll climb out along the iron and pull him on board. Can you manage?"

"Simple," said Alec. "I'll just keep my foot on the brake. But will you be OK?"

"Nothing to it," said Ginger, sliding feet first through the opening in the window and on to the girder. He loped like a cat over the first six feet. Then he stopped and pointed down.

"Hey, here comes the cavalry."

Sure enough, Mr Hardcastle and the other men, followed by PC Hadley, were over the canal and running towards the crane house. Alec placed his foot firmly on the brake lever and watched Ginger as he reached a point on the girder next to Councillor Blaggett and sat down astride it. Then Ginger reached out with both hands to grasp the huge, sodden man under his armpits.

Alec watched them so keenly that he never heard the door behind him crash open and the sound of feet lumbering across the floor. The next moment he was seized by the collar and dragged away from the winding drum. As he was jerked backwards, his foot struck the brake.

"Now you've done it," said one of the men.

Freed of the brake, the drum began to roll. Outside on the girder Ginger sat with arms outstretched, but Councillor Blaggett, with a groan of regret, was slowly winding and rattling down into the queasy depths of the canal.

Mr Hardcastle let go of Alec's collar as the three men bumped into one another, while attempting to put matters right. Alec tried to reach the brake lever, barging into one of the council men. He grasped it at last and pulled, but it would not lock. The chain continued to run. Blaggett was up to his chest in the canal and sinking, his white smeared face turned up to the sky.

"Oh, he'll drown this time," thought Alec. But he couldn't hold that brake lever.

Right at that moment, a large oil-stained hand appeared next to Alec's, grasping the metal rod.

"All right, son, you can let go now."

Alec looked up in bewilderment.

It was Dad.

15

Dad Makes a Speech

Alec stared. How did that happen? There were Dad
and one of his mates from the railway, still in their
peaked caps and jackets. As Alec slipped to one
side, they moved in and jammed on the brake lever.

They were just in time, for the councillor was
now barely visible above the mud and slime, though
his hands still desperately clung to the chain. Dad
and his mate slowly began to winch the councillor
up again. They took it very gently, easing the heavy
body up, until Blaggett was half-in and half-out of
the water.

Dad turned to Mr Hardcastle.

"Here, make yourself useful. Go and get a rope."

Without a word, Mr Hardcastle ran out of the
door.

Dad shouted through the window to Ginger.

"Hey, lad. Can you hear me all right?"

Ginger looked round and nodded.

"Listen. You'll never pull him on to the girder.
He's too heavy. He'll have you off. Now here's
what we'll do." Dad reached for the rope which
Mr Hardcastle was holding, made a swift loop on
one end, and then leaned forward to the window.

"Can you catch this rope, lad?"

"OK," shouted Ginger.

The rope shot through the air and Ginger caught it first try. "Now, put that loop over the end of the crane arm, can you?" Ginger gave the thumbs-up sign.

Dad turned again to Mr Hardcastle and the policeman. "Now you lot, go down to the canal bank. While we hold the chain fast up here, you take the end of this rope down there. Then you swing the crane arm round and draw Old Blaggett over to the side. Make sure you get a good grip on him. He'll weigh a ton. And maybe one of you'd better go and get some blankets and brandy."

From then on, things went smoothly. Dad and his mate kept the chain drum steady, holding Blaggett just clear of the canal, while Mr Hardcastle and the others pulled on the rope, which swivelled the crane arm round and slowly landed the exhausted man in the arms of his assistant and PC Hadley on the towpath.

"All right, Bill," said Dad, "we'll wind her in now."

They spun the winding drum and the chain rattled up to rest. Dad waved his arm for Ginger to come back along the girder and gave him a hand as he slid back through the window.

"You're a brave lad, but you wouldn't have been safe trying to hold him. He'd have had you in the Cut as well as himself. But, Alec lad, what was the old fool doing in the canal? We were bringing the

3.30 into the station, and Bill here looked down from the viaduct and there was Blaggett going in and out of the canal like a yo-yo. I've never seen ought like it before in my life. If it hadn't been dangerous, I'd have had a good laugh."

Bill grinned. "I expect they'll have a good laugh up at the Club about it, anyway."

Alec quickly told his father about what had happened, leaving out the earlier part of the story about Abu and the beer can. He didn't feel Dad would be ready to swallow that at this stage. Dad heard it all and nodded grimly.

"And Blaggett reckoned there was an illegal immigrant here in the Tank, did he? Well, there's one born every minute. Anyway, there's no one here now, is there? Though . . ." Dad looked strangely at Alec, "someone's left their blanket here on the table. We'd best take it with us and find out who it belongs to."

Down on the canal bank Councillor Blaggett, well wrapped up and his colour restored by a glass of brandy, was sitting against the crane house wall. He looked up as the four of them approached.

"They tell me you saved my life, Harold Bowden." Dad snorted.

"It was these two lads, our Alec and his mate, who saved you. And that bright spark," Dad nodded towards Hardcastle, "nearly did you in with his helping hand." He bent down and squatted by Blaggett. "How are you feeling now?"

"I'm all right now, thank you," replied Blaggett rather pompously.

"You ought to have more sense at your age, climbing on girders like a monkey, chasing imaginary black men through the shrubbery."

Councillor Blaggett looked furious.

"You may laugh, Harold Bowden, but it is no laughing matter. There has been an illegal immigrant in this area, probably the source of illness we had reported from Boner's Street last week, and though I appreciate what these two lads have done, they are very much involved in the whole business."

Ginger was furious. "There wasn't any illness like that in Boner's Street. It was just me with the flu."

"I think you should be careful what you're saying," said Blaggett. "The constable here is looking into your activities, as well as the activities of young Bowden there." Councillor Blaggett looked up at PC Hadley, but the constable appeared to be making a careful examination of a fly on the wall.

"Now, look here, Joe Blaggett," Dad's face suddenly became red. Alec had never seen him look like that before. "I think it's about time someone talked straight to you because you're going to end up making this town a laughing stock."

The councillor started to speak, but Dad didn't even notice.

"There's hardly a week goes by, without you making some daft statement or other. And this week, you've hit the jackpot."

"What d'you mean, Harold Bowden?"

Dad folded his arms. That's funny, thought Alec, that's just what Mum does before she's going to blast somebody.

"Why don't you, for once in your life, Joe Blaggett, do something really useful? Instead of pushing around those people down in Boner's Street, why don't you go down there and find out what they want? Find out if they want to be shunted off to Moorside? In fact you don't need to. Just go home and ask your own missus if she wants to go out to Moorside. And instead of chasing black men through this dump, why don't you have a proper look round Boner's and Upshaw and those other streets? There's room for more homes down there, for Bugletown people. And those houses in Boner's Street could be fixed up and decent homes made out of them. In fact, there's a lot that could be done to smarten up the place and make it comfortable."

Dad raised his hand.

"Look, I know you're not responsible for the whole issue, but you do pull a lot of weight. So why not pull it in the right direction for a change?"

Dad stopped suddenly, as though he were astonished with himself. Alec looked at him in awe. He thought to himself, I won't forget this for a long time, and I'll bet Councillor Blaggett won't either.

There came a hooting from beyond the big gate.

"Ah, that'll be the ambulance," said PC Hadley.

"We'll be off, then, our Alec," said Dad.

They all walked together towards the gate. The ambulance men passed them on the way down to the canal with a stretcher for Councillor Blaggett. As they passed, one called out:

"Hey, Harold. How did he manage to get into the canal?"

Dad shook his head.

"It's a long story, Fred."

"I'll look out for you in the Three Fiddlers at the weekend, and you can tell us then. It must be good."

"Why, it's almost unbelievable," said Dad.

At the gate Alec turned to Ginger. "I'll come over and see you later, Ginge. OK?"

Ginger shook his head.

"No, best not come over." He jerked his head back at the Tank. "One of these bright boys might have his eye on you. I'll see you tomorrow in school. Tara."

"Tara," said Alec and Ginger loped off.

"Who's that boy?" said Dad.

"That's Ginger Wallace from school. Our Kim knows his mother from the biscuit works."

"Oh," said Dad, and left it at that.

By the allotments, they parted company with Dad's mate and walked on towards home.

Alec suddenly remembered something.

"Dad?"

"What is it, son?"

"How did you manage to get down into the Tank so quickly? You couldn't have come round by the High Road."

Dad looked embarrassed. Then he laughed and said:

"Ask your mum."

Alec looked disbelieving, but Dad repeated, "Ask your mum."

And they walked the rest of the way in silence.

Mum was at the gate talking to neighbours when they arrived. News travels fast, and she already had an idea what had happened. The rest of the story came out over tea with Mum and Kim, who had already arrived home, laughing till the tears came.

When Alec got a chance, he put in a word.

"Mum, Dad said I was to ask you how he got down into the Tank so quickly from the viaduct."

Mum shot an outraged glance at Dad, who looked up at the ceiling. Then Mum laughed.

"He would. Oh, he would."

"Oh, go on, Mum, tell us," begged Alec.

"I'm not sure I will. It's private," said Mum, but she was still smiling.

"Oh, go on, our Mum. He's a big lad now," said Kim teasingly.

"Oh, all right," said Mum. "Your dad knows a short cut down from the railway into the Tank, down the side of the viaduct. You probably can't see it now because of all those elder bushes."

Dad hid a smile behind his hand.

"But, how, Mum. How do you . . .?"

"Well, Alec, during the war, they used to make tanks in Bugletown Ordnance. That's why people called it the Tank, the name stuck to it. Well, after the war I worked there. Your dad was on the

143

railway along with Granddad. We weren't married then, and what with shift work and all, we didn't see all that much of each other. So . . ."

"Oh, I know," said Alec, "Dad used to sneak down the path from the railway, and you'd meet him down by the canal."

Mum blushed. Kim chuckled.

"There you are, our Alec. The romantic past of the Bowden family."

But Alec had other things on his mind.

"Mum?"

"Yes?"

"Whereabouts did you work in the Tank?"

Now Mum began to laugh.

"Where do you think, Alec? Where do you think?"

Alec looked baffled.

"In the crane house, of course. How do you think your dad knew how to operate that crane?"

Alec's mouth fell open. Kim laughed outright.

"You've shocked him now, our Mum. He'll never hold his head up again. His mother was a crane driver."

They all burst out laughing. What a fantastic end to a fantastic day.

16

Abu Puts in a Disappearance

But there was more excitement at home that night. A reporter and photographer from the *Bugletown Gazette* came round. The reporter, whose uncle worked in the goods yards, knew Dad slightly and there was a good deal of talk about Councillor Blaggett, Boner's Street and the Tank. They didn't leave until the big teapot, usually brought out on Sundays, had been emptied twice. Dad, Mum and Kim sat round the front-room table with the *Gazette* people; Alec sat on the window ledge and listened to the talk. Mum kept sending him meaningful glances, but didn't say anything about homework.

As the journalists left, Alec burst out,

"Aren't you going to interview Ginger Wallace?"

The reporter grinned.

"We'll be down at Boner's Street tomorrow night, Alec. This is a big story. Front page stuff. Besides," he whispered, "I couldn't take any more tea this evening."

Next day at school Eulalia passed Alec a note.

Ronnie Carter muttered, "Why can't I get notes from smashing women?"

Eulalia heard him and smiled sweetly.

"Because I'm particular who I talk to, Fat-face."

Alec managed to open the note just as first lesson started. "All OK till the weekend. But have to do something drastic then. Salaam from Abu."

Alec took the note as a hint and, apart from a brief nod to Ginger in the yard at lunch break, he made no more contact. He relied on Ginger and Eulalia to look after Abu. But it was still worrying. In a day or two the weekend would be here and he hadn't a clue what they could do. He'd heard in a telly programme that you could get fake passports in the Portobello Road in London. Or was it driving licences? He wasn't sure, and he didn't know how to get to the Portobello Road anyway. And what did you do when you got there? Did you walk along, saying out of the corner of your mouth, "How much for a passport for a materialized genie?" Or did you get a slip of paper under your glass in a bar with the address of a backroom over a barber's shop?

He didn't know that either. He'd never been in a bar and he didn't go near barber's shops any more often than he had to. No, he wasn't really trained for emergencies like this. Now, if only he could give his old beer can a rub, and say, "I want a passport, work permit and insurance cards for a genie who has entered the country illegally." No, he didn't know what to do, but he knew one thing. If there was something he could do to help Abu, even if it were something you weren't supposed to do, he'd do it like a shot.

"And where is Mr Bowden now? At the Court of Saladin?"

The mock polite tones of Tweedy Harris brought him back to earth. It was mid-afternoon and he was halfway through a history lesson. What were they doing? Was it the Hundred Years War, or the wool trade? His mind did several hundred revs to the second, but came up with nothing.

"Er – I was just thinking about what you said, sir."

"Very flattering. And what did I say?"

"That's what I was thinking."

The class rocked. Tweedy, for once in a mild humour, smiled as well.

The rest of the day slipped away. Nothing disastrous happened, though Alec almost wished it had. He was beginning to know the meaning of the expression "the suspense is killing me".

Just after tea that evening, Alec was sitting in the caravan with Granddad, sharing a bag of crisps, when Granddad pointed and said, "Who's that young feller, just going up to the back door?"

Alec peered through the caravan window. He recognized the young coin-collector in the leather jacket, right away.

"It's Arthur Blaggett, Councillor Blaggett's son," he said.

Granddad looked anxious.

"What does he want? Is he spying things out?"

"After a word with our Kim, more like," said Alec. "I'll sneak up to the corner and have a listen, shall I?"

Granddad shrugged. Alec nipped out of the caravan and crept up to the corner of the coalhouse from where he could hear without being seen. It was worth it.

Arthur Blaggett knocked and waited. After a second Dad stood in the door. He looked grim.

"And what do you want?"

That wasn't like Dad. He was usually a bit more friendly than that. Arthur Blaggett looked nervous. Alec rubbed his hands joyfully.

"It's my dad like," said Arthur Blaggett. "He wants to see you."

"I'm not sure any member of my family wants to see any member of your family at the moment."

Arthur wriggled inside his leather jacket.

"Well, Mr Bowden. Dad only asked me, if I'd ask you, if you'd be good enough to, I mean . . ."

Dad gave him no help at all. "No, I don't know what you mean."

"He wants you to go round with him to Boner's Street to talk to the people there. He reckons that'll help."

"He wants me to do his dirty work for him, does he?"

"Oh, no, Mr Bowden." Arthur's voice went so far up the scale that Alec became alarmed.

"No, he told me to say that he were – he was very interested in what you'd said and . . . er . . ."

From the kitchen behind Dad, Alec could hear Kim's voice.

"Our Dad, don't torment the lad so. Tell him yes or no."

Arthur Blaggett tried to peer round Dad, which took some doing since Dad was broad.

"Oh, er, hallo, Kim."

Alec could see the corner of Dad's mouth twitching.

"Tell Councillor Blaggett that if he'd like to see me, on a purely social basis of course, I shall be in the Railway Club at nine o'clock tonight." Dad paused. "He can ask for me at the door."

"Oh, thanks very much, Mr Bowden." Arthur Blaggett stood there. Dad looked at him.

"Well, was there something else?"

"I was just wondering . . ."

"Oh, Dad, you are a pest," came Kim's voice.

"Ask him in, Harold," Mum intervened at last. Alec wasn't sure, but he had the feeling that she was having a quiet laugh too.

Arthur Blaggett disappeared along with Dad into the kitchen, and Alec went quietly back into the caravan where Granddad had a can of beer open.

"Would you like a sup, Alec?"

"No, thanks, Granddad. I don't like beer."

The old man looked mischievous.

"But I thought you did."

"How do you mean?"

"Well, I've seen you carrying your empties about, that's all."

"What empties?"

"That old beer can you wouldn't let your mum put in the dustbin."

Without thinking, Alec put his hand in his pocket. That was funny. The can wasn't there.

Come to think, he hadn't seen it since yesterday. He must have left it somewhere.

He felt a sudden pang of regret and disappointment. The can had no magic power any more, but he'd become very attached to it. He'd got used to it sitting in his pocket, like an old friend.

"Eh, Alec?" Granddad was looking at him.

"Oh, ah. That old beer can."

"Yes, that old beer can. You're starting early, aren't you? I never supped ale before I was fourteen and I started work at thirteen. This is what they call the permissive society, eh?"

Alec shrugged.

"Oh, it never had any beer in it. I just picked it up."

"Whatever for, Alec?"

"Well, a sort of good luck thing, that's all."

"And did it bring you any luck?"

"I'm not sure, Granddad. I don't know whether to believe in things like good luck, or not."

"Oh, I don't know, lad, never say die. You never know what's round the corner. Anyway, you've had a good week, this week. Interviews and all. I expect they'll have your picture in the paper: 'Boy hero of Bugletown. Large councillor saved from fate worse than death.'"

Alec laughed, though it was really not funny. So many things had happened since that day he had picked up the can at the corner of Boner's Street. So many fantastic things had taken place. It was hard to believe it had all come and gone in the space of just over a fortnight. He looked at

Granddad supping his beer. Granddad would never know what had upset his caravan that night.

And he, Alec, could never tell him, because it just wasn't believable. Nor were the Arabian feasts in his bedroom, the slippers, the silver coins, the Great Itch, or the tremendous transformation of Boner's Street and the Tank, which had only lasted seconds.

All the same, he mused, perhaps some good has come of it all, if Councillor Blaggett's having second thoughts about clearing Miss Morris and the Wallaces and the other people out of Boner's Street. And now Dad was on the warpath, as well. That was a transformation of sorts. Perhaps there was real magic in the can . . .

Then he remembered, there was Abu. Abu, not in the spirit but in the flesh, all six foot ten of him, or thereabouts. And to think, he'd once fitted right inside that little beer can. Still, didn't Mr Jameson once say that there was enough energy in a cup of water to drive an ocean liner to New York and back? Or was it a drop of water? He couldn't remember. But it was a fantastic idea, all that energy there, waiting to be released.

Granddad looked out of the window.

"There's your dad off to the Club. Hey, and look, somebody else is off somewhere, too."

Alec peeped out.

Kim, towing Arthur Blaggett behind her, was walking off round the side of the house.

"Where will they be off to?" said Granddad.

"The Odeon, late show, I should think."

"Maybe. That's a funny thing, now. That's the

last family in Bugletown I thought we'd ever have anything to do with. I remember Joe Blaggett's father at school. I gave him a black eye once."

"What was that for, Granddad?"

"Oh, I forget now. These days I can't remember what I had for dinner."

The old man looked after Kim and Arthur Blaggett as they disappeared up the road. He chuckled.

> *"This is my daughter's wedding day.*
> *Ten thousand pounds I'll give away.*
> *On second thoughts, I think it best,*
> *To put it back in the old oak chest."*

"Oh, you are daft, Granddad," said Alec.

"I know, lad, but handsome with it. Hey, what's this, Alec? This place is like High Street on Market Day tonight."

"What do you mean, Granddad?"

"There's a black boy and girl out there in the entry. What do they want?"

Alec jumped to his feet.. Something was wrong. Eulalia and Ginger would never have come up here, just like that.

"See you, Granddad," he called out hastily, as he tore open the caravan door and tumbled down the steps.

Ginger and Eulalia stood by the corner of the back yard. Their faces were serious.

"What's happened?" said Alec.

"It's Abu. We can't find him anywhere. He's just gone."

152

17

Ma'asalaama!

"Gone?" said Alec.

Eulalia nodded.

"He was in our back room. Dad was working out what we could do about him, but I think Abu was a bit bothered about troubling us."

"That's right," said Ginger. "When he knew the law could get really nasty over things like this."

"Do you mean, he just walked out, like that?"

"Well, we were all watching something on the box in the front room tonight, Abu was in the back room. Mum gave him his tea earlier on and he decided to have a sleep."

"That figures," said Alec. "His favourite occupation."

"When we went in to see him later on, he'd just disappeared. But where can he have got to? He's got no money. He can't go anywhere."

"Oh, yes he can," said Alec.

"Where?" they both spoke together.

"A pound to a penny, back to the Tank."

"You could be right," said Ginger. "Come on, then."

They set off at a run, out of the yard, down the

road and past the allotments. They reached the plank fence round the Tank in two minutes flat.

"They were quick to put the padlock on again," said Eulalia.

"Yes," said Alec, as he walked slowly along the fence. "And, this time, they've done a proper job. They've nailed up all the loose planks. We can't get through."

"Come on then, round to Boner's Street," said Ginger.

"Don't waste your time," called his sister. "They'll have nailed up the other side as well."

"Dad came down the back way from the railway viaduct the other day," said Alec.

"That's risky," said Eulalia. "That means going over the wall by the Railway Club."

"There's only one thing for it, then," said Ginger.

"What's that?"

"Over the top."

"But it must be twelve feet at least," said Alec, "and there's nothing to hold on to on this side."

"There's a ladder with some scaffolding at the top of the slope," said a voice behind them.

All three jumped. Granddad stood there. "If you're dead set on getting over there to find your friend, I'll keep watch for you."

Ginger looked suspiciously at Granddad.

"What friend?"

Granddad made a face.

"You can fool Councillor Blaggett, but you can't fool me. Hetty Morris told me there was a big black man going through the fence into the Tank. Now I know she sees funny things at night, but she misses nothing that goes on in daylight."

"You won't tell, will you?" pleaded Eulalia.

Granddad sniffed.

"If I wanted to tell, I'd have split on you before now. Don't be daft."

Eulalia grinned at him.

"You're smashing."

He grinned back, showing the gaps in his teeth.

"You're all right yourself."

"Come on," said Ginger. "Let's get that ladder."

It took no more than a couple of minutes to carry the ladder down to the fence and set it up. On the other side there were cross planks which made the job of climbing down easier.

The bridge, repaired during the siege of the crane house, was intact, and they crossed it quickly and headed for the main Tank building. Their footsteps sounded very loud in the still evening. It was getting late now and, though it was summer, the sun was moving down the sky and the buildings cast long, weird shadows.

"This is a spooky place," said Eulalia. "I can't see why Abu wanted to come back here."

"Well, he's a spirit himself," said Ginger.

"No, he's not," said Alec indignantly, "He's a genie, Third Class, one of the original slaves of the lamp."

"Much good it's done him," retorted Ginger. He stopped as they reached the foot of the crane room stairs.

"Hey, think of that. A slave for nine hundred years. Doing what you're told for nine centuries. Catch me doing that for nine hundred seconds," said Ginger.

"You wait till our Ma hears what you said," laughed Eulalia. "She'll wave her hand, and you'll say, 'What is thy will, O master?'"

"Huh," replied her brother and led the way up the stairs. They entered the crane room in a rush, calling for Abu. Their voices echoed round the old building, but the room was quite empty.

"He must be somewhere else in the Tank," said Eulalia.

Alec shook his head.

"No, this is the only place with a proper roof on it. If he's not in the crane room, he must be away somewhere."

He looked unhappily round the room, now half lost in the dusk. The old table, upset during the struggle over the crane brake lever, had been set upright again. The paper bag, which held Abu's sandwiches, still lay on the floor. But there was no sign of his old friend.

"Hey, what's that over in the corner, there?" said Ginger.

"Where?"

"Over by the far wall."

Alec and Eulalia looked, but could see nothing. Then a last ray from the setting sun, slanting through the broken windows, caught the corner and drew a quick glint of metal from it. Alec dived towards it.

"It's my can. I thought I'd lost it." He picked it up and wiped it on his jumper sleeve. It had become grimy again from lying in the corner. He must have put it down the other day, when they were messing about with the crane, and forgotten about it. He polished it lovingly.

"Hey, you really love that old bit of tin," said Eulalia.

"Sentimental reasons," replied Alec, "This was Abu's home, remember? Now he's got none."

He put the can down and the three of them stood round it.

Eulalia put one arm on Alec's shoulder and the other on Ginger's.

Ginger said, "It doesn't seem real any more. Did you really rub on that tin and he came out, just like that?"

"Oh, he didn't come out in that way. He just spoke and that's how I knew he was there. That is, until that day when I tried my super spell and because it was too much for him, he appeared."

"How did you do it? Show us," said Eulalia.

Alec cleared his throat. He rubbed his finger round the top of the can and said, "Salaam Aleikum, O Abu Salem." His voice sounded funny and Eulalia looked at him with a smile.

"Well, he's not there any more, in spirit or in flesh," said Ginger.

Suddenly Alec had an idea.

"Say it with me."

"Say what?" They stared at him.

"Say, with me, 'Salaam'."

157

They shrugged, "OK."

Ginger put his arm on Alec's shoulder. All three of them bent over the can and together they said solemnly and loudly,

"Salaam Aleikum, O Abu Salem."

"Again," said Alec.

"Salaam Aleikum, O Abu Salem."

"And a last time, but louder," he urged.

"Salaam Aleikum, O Abu Salem," they called.

From the can on the table came a tinny sound, like a transistor with a sore throat.

"Salaam Aleikum, O Alec."

"Listen, Abu," said Alec. "Ginger's here and Eulalia. We've been worried stiff about you. We thought you were lost somewhere."

"Not lost, but found, O friends of mine."

"How did it happen?"

"Today as I ate the fried chicken, given me by the good Mrs Wallace, I felt my old power begin to return, though at first only feebly. So, remembering what is written in the Book of Magic, I lay down to sleep. In my sleep the power came back to me and I returned to my resting place . . . until I was awoken."

"No need to be sarky, Abu," said Alec. "But now that you're safe in there, what happens?"

"Nothing, O Alec. I must sleep for another hundred years, I think, to recover strength."

"Oh, no," they shouted, "not a hundred years."

"A long, long time."

"But can't you come back and see us?" pleaded Alec.

"Maybe, some day," came the reply, now growing fainter. "I fear that the laws of your land have no room for me. Perhaps, some day. Now, may Allah protect you, good friends. Ma'asalaama . . ." and the voice faded right away. The crane room was silent. At the same time the light began to fade and it grew colder.

Alec shivered. Eulalia said,

"That was sad, but no good staying here. Let's go home."

Ginger nodded. Alec picked up the can and put it into his pocket. They went down the stairs together and walked across to the canal and the plank bridge.

Climbing the fence in near darkness was tricky, but the ladder was still in position on the other side. They climbed over and carried it back to where the council men had left their scaffolding planks and poles. Then they walked up the slope to the top near Alec's home, and stood together for a while.

It was all over now, thought Alec.

Abu had gone. That was a disaster. Despite all the trouble, he was going to miss Abu a lot. Then he looked at Eulalia and Ginger. He'd lost a genie, but found two new friends. That was a triumph. You could call it a draw, disasters one, triumphs one. Without being aware of it, he thought aloud.

"If we had extra time, we might win."

Eulalia and Ginger stared at him, then both burst out laughing.

"Skinny, you're crazy," they said. Then they waved at him and set off into the gathering darkness.

As they went, Ginger's voice came back to Alec. "See you in school tomorrow."

"OK," shouted Alec. He turned towards the side entry of his house. He could see his mother talking to Granddad by the light from the door of the caravan.

"You're late, our Alec. So straight upstairs now."

Alec didn't argue. He didn't feel like saying anything. He walked through the kitchen and climbed the stairs to his room. Once inside, he sat down on his bed and looked around him. His own room.

Perhaps, now that Dad was stirring things up, there might be a chance that Tom and Elaine could find a place nearer home, and maybe he wouldn't have to move up into the boxroom after all. If he had any luck, that is . . .

He started to get undressed. The can in his jeans pocket knocked against his leg.

He took it out and was just about to put it away in his cupboard, when he lifted it up to his ear.

He thought, he couldn't be sure, but he thought he heard a faint sound. Not like surf on a distant shore, but snoring on a nearby bed.

Alec grinned happily.

"Ma'asalaama, Abu, wherever you are."